# ENCORE

# Hollywood Daughters

## A Family Trilogy

# ENCORE

## Joan Lowery Nixon

BANTAM BOOKS

NEW YORK • TORONTO • LONDON • SYDNEY • AUCKLAND

ENCORE

A Bantam Book / October 1990

Produced by Daniel Weiss Associates, Inc.,
33 West 17th Street,
New York, NY 10011

Book design by Richard Oriolo

**Library of Congress Cataloging-in-Publication Data**
Nixon, Joan Lowery.
Encore / by Joan Lowery Nixon.
p.    cm. — (Hollywood daughters)
Summary: Cassie's daughter Erin, who identifies closely with her
grandmother Abby, wants to be an actress more than anything in
the world, but is disappointed that her parents do not approve of
her working in the television medium.
ISBN 0-553-07024-X
[1. Actors and actresses—Fiction.   2. Mothers and daughters—
Fiction.   3. Hollywood (Los Angeles, Calif.)—Fiction.]   I. Title.
II. Series: Nixon, Joan Lowery.   Hollywood daughters.
PZ7.N65En   1990
[Fic]—dc20                                                    90-30128
                                                                 CIP
                                                                  AC

Published simultaneously in the United States and Canada

PRINTED IN THE UNITED STATES OF AMERICA

BVG        0   9   8   7   6   5   4   3   2   1

*For Pili Hanson*

# ENCORE

"*R*oll sound . . . Roll camera . . . Mark it!" The slate snapped, and the disembodied voice behind the portable lights that glared in Erin Jenkins's eyes called, "Action!"

Erin ran across the set of *The Family Next Door* and flung herself on the pink flowered sofa, while her pretty, dark-haired television mother, Lydia Crawford, assumed an expression of gentle patience.

"Mom!" Erin snatched up a pillow and hugged it in anguish. "I'm never going to speak to Clarence again. Ever! He lied to me, and I hate him!"

"*Hate*'s a pretty strong word, isn't it, Katie?" Lydia smiled sympathetically as she spoke.

Erin buried her chin in the pillow. "Well, maybe I don't exactly *hate* him, but if he fell over a cliff I wouldn't cry about it."

Lydia put an arm around Erin's shoulders and snuggled her close. "It might not be as bad as you think it is. Have you given Clarence a chance to explain?"

"How could he explain?" Erin sat upright, facing her TV mother. "Clarence told me he had to take a piano lesson, but I saw him eating ice cream with that new girl in our class."

Marcie Lane, in her role as Katie Norman's glamorous big sister, Andrea, crossed the set and perched on the arm of the sofa. She smiled lazily, tossed back her long, silver-gold hair, and in an amused tone asked, "Is this new girl pretty?"

"Pretty? To one frog, another frog is pretty!" Erin waited one beat for the audience reaction the line would get. "Yes, she's pretty, and she's blond. I suppose you're going to say that blondes have more fun."

Marcie studied the fingernails on her right hand. "Maybe not more fun, but they do seem to get more ice cream."

Erin gave an exasperated sigh to allow time for laughter. "Go away, Andrea," she said. "Mom and I were talking about . . . men." She rested comfortably against Lydia, who patted Erin's shoulder and brushed her hair back from her forehead.

"Men? I'd hardly call Clarence a man," Marcie said. "His idea of a big date is to pick you up on his bicycle and take you to Sears to watch them carmel the popcorn."

"Now, Andrea—" Lydia began.

At the same time, Erin indignantly sputtered, "I suppose you think—"

"Cut." John Haywood's deep voice boomed over the intercom from the control room. "You stepped on Lydia's line, Erin."

"Sorry, guys," Erin said. "I'm really sorry."

Lydia gave Erin's shoulder a sympathetic squeeze, and Erin smiled at her gratefully.

Jake Barlow, the tall, handsome actor who played Marcie's current boyfriend on the situation comedy, moved onto the set and grinned at Erin. "No problem, babe," he said. "We all make mistakes."

Erin looked up in surprise. Jake, who'd been on the show less than two months, had rarely paid attention to her.

Marcie instantly stepped between them to clutch Jake's hand. "We were supposed to wrap this up before five, and now we'll be working late," she snapped at Erin. "You've been jumpy and blowing your lines all afternoon. What's the matter with you?"

"I said I was sorry." Erin couldn't tell Marcie the reason, and she couldn't feel less sisterly to the tall, beautiful girl who lorded it over her on and off the set.

Marcie and Erin were both seventeen, but to Erin's

irritation Marcie looked at least two years older, and Erin looked younger than her age. Marcie played Andrea Norman, the beautiful high-school senior who had boys lining up for dates. Erin was Katie, the cute, hazel-eyed, curly-haired, pug-nosed teenager who yearned to lead a life as exciting as her big sister's. So far, her only date was awkward Clarence Nutweilder, who wore stiffly starched and ironed short-sleeved shirts, polyester slacks that didn't reach his ankles, white socks, and black oxfords.

"It's just so inconvenient," Marcie said.

The way things were going, Erin didn't need to be scolded by Marcie. She glared at her.

John spoke again from the booth. "Let it go, Marcie. Everyone has an off day once in a while." He addressed his assistant director, who stood at the edge of the set. "Dave, let's take a short break."

The boom operator swung the boom mike up and away from the set, and the gaffer turned off the hot lights.

Five-year-old Tina Reed, her curls bouncing, ran to Erin and took her hand. "It's all right, Erin. Everybody makes mistakes. I even made a mistake once," she said.

Marcie snickered, and Tina glanced at her, her face troubled. Erin bent to Tina and whispered, "Don't pay attention to Marcie. We don't like her, do we?"

"No, we don't." Tina turned her back to Marcie and moved closer to Erin, who hugged her.

Marcie stretched, her blouse pulling taut over her full breasts. Some of the crew stared, which Erin knew was exactly what Marcie wanted. "Only two more weeks," Marcie said, "and we'll be through taping. I did tell you that I'm cast in a Franklin Nast film, didn't I? It will be going into production in April." Marcie's voice was a satisfied purr.

"What's the film called?" Lydia asked.

"*I Was A Teenaged Dork,*" Erin chanted, striking a monster pose.

Everyone but Marcie laughed, Erin included, but Erin was unhappy because Marcie had a job to walk into and she hadn't. Erin was the better actress, but Marcie got the offers.

"The working title is *Spyscraper,*" Marcie said. With one hand, she flipped back her long hair again. "It's a wild comedy about a foreign spy in New York City who has a romantic entanglement with a cocktail waitress. Light stuff, but my agent said it's going to be terrific exposure."

"Isn't that up to the costume department?" Erin guessed that Marcie had got the part because she could look like a bimbo, and she was comforted by the thought.

Marcie ignored Erin. "I've heard rumors that *The Dorchesters* has been optioned by Orion," she went on. "When it's cast, I want to be ready for it. *Spyscraper* will keep me in the public eye."

"What's *The Dorchesters*?" Erin asked, curious in spite of herself.

"A fantastic new novel," Lydia answered before Marcie could. "I'm reading it now, and crying all the way through it."

Gene McMillan, the broad-shouldered, jovial father of *The Family Next Door,* arrived on the set. "Well, this is a big night for Erin and her family," he said with a wink in Erin's direction. "The illustrious Abby Grant's new variety show is premiering tonight."

Marcie was clearly annoyed at this shift in the conversation. "I'd hardly call it a premiere," she sniffed. "When they use the word *premiere,* it means they're planning other shows to follow. According to the critics, Abby Grant's show is not going to get off the ground."

"They're wrong, and you're wrong!" Erin felt her cheeks burning as she took a step toward Marcie.

"I agree," Gene said. He wrapped an arm around Erin's shoulders, effectively holding her in place. "Abby's the queen, and all of us in Hollywood are her loyal subjects."

"She hasn't had a show in years," Marcie scoffed.

"She hasn't needed one!" Erin retorted. She hated feeling so defensive. She'd never admit to Marcie—to anyone— that she *was* scared about how her grandmother's show would be received. Abby would never admit it, either, but it was pretty obvious to Erin that her grandmother was scared, too. Abby had always done situation comedy and felt at home with the format, but this show . . .

As though she were reading Erin's mind, Lydia said smoothly, "Abby will be fantastic. A variety show is made to order for her."

Erin smiled gratefully at Lydia. "Abby's lined up some terrific guest stars, and—"

"Stars who are as old as she is," Marcie interrupted.

"Actors who have reached the top," Gene interjected. "Where we'd all like to be. Right?"

John stepped between Erin and Marcie, repositioning Marcie by grasping her shoulders and walking her backward to the edge of the set. "Actors, take your places. Everyone else, clear the set," he said. "We'll run through this scene from the top. This will be a take."

Gene patted Erin's arm and whispered, "Don't let Marcie get to you, Erin. When you lose your composure, you give her just what she wants."

"Okay. I'll try," Erin whispered back. She found her mark and took three deep breaths, steadying herself. "No mistakes this time," she said to John. "I promise."

"Good," he said. He paused and looked at his watch. "When we're through here, how about all of us going across the street to Roscoe and Ruby's, ordering some burgers, and watching Abby's show on their TV?"

"Count me in," Gene said.

Lydia hesitated only an instant before she smiled at Erin. "I'd like that," she said.

Tina glanced hopefully toward her mother, who sat next to Annie Blevins, their studio teacher, at the side of the set. Mrs. Reed, a thin, hawk-nosed woman who constantly hovered over her daughter, put down her knitting needles, preparing for the quiet needed on the set, and shook her head. "Past your bedtime," she mouthed.

Tina's forehead puckered, and her eyes threatened to fill with tears, but Erin could see the little girl struggle with her feelings and win. Tina closed her eyes, and when she opened them she was back in character as Amy Norman, the perky, bubbling, youngest daughter of the family.

*She's a real pro,* Erin thought with admiration. She wondered if she could have handled the turndown without tears if she'd been an actress at Tina's age.

Erin had always known that someday she'd be an actress. She'd been entranced with her grandmother, wanted to be exactly like her, and she'd spent hours dressing up in anything she could find to pretend that she, too, was a star.

Sometimes it had gotten her into trouble.

There was the evening—was she four or was she five? —when she'd swept haughtily into the den where her mother was having coffee with Abby.

That night, Cassie was dressed in something shimmery and blue. Erin liked to look at her beautiful mother. She was soft and lovely, like satin pillows and white flowers and the slippery binding on Erin's favorite pink blanket. Abby, on the other hand, was as demure as a stoplight in a blouse and pants as bright and cheerful as her red-red lipstick.

"What in the world are you doing with that chain of paper clips draped around your neck?" Erin's mother had asked with a smile.

Erin had lifted her chin a notch higher and scornfully replied, "These are not paper clips, darling. This is my diamond necklace."

Cassie had stared with surprise and murmured, "Erin, don't be rude!"

"She's not being rude," Abby had told Cassie. "She's just pretending."

Erin had climbed onto her grandmother's lap and twined the chain of paper clips around one finger. "I'm not pretending," she'd explained. "I'm acting."

Abby had chuckled with delight, but Cassie had avoided her mother's eyes and said, "Erin, I think it's about time we introduced you to some new activities. How would you like to take piano lessons?"

"No, thank you," Erin had said, hoping if she were polite enough her mother would drop the idea of piano lessons. She'd snuggled against her grandmother's chest, enjoying being wrapped in Abby's arms. "I'd rather be an actress. On Abby's show."

"Absolutely not!" Cassie's face had reddened with embarrassment at the urgency in her words. "Erin, I want you to have a childhood, not a career," she explained more evenly.

"Why?"

"Because I said so. That's why."

"Why don't we write in a small part for Erin in one of the episodes?" Abby suggested. "Something not much more than a walk-on. It would be fun for her, and you could hardly call that a career."

"The answer is *no*." Cassie stood and looked down at them, adding firmly, "For both of you." She held out a hand to Erin. "Come on, sweetheart. It's time for your bath and bedtime story."

But Erin hadn't given up. She knew what she wanted, and she knew that Abby was on her side.

"There's a lot you're going to have to learn," Abby had told her. After that, she had begun to give Erin pointers.

One afternoon, when Abby had returned from a three-week engagement in Las Vegas, Erin had put on an impromptu stand-up routine for her. Abby had laughed until tears came to her eyes. "You've got what it takes, sweetheart," she'd told Erin. "If you're willing to match the talent with hard work, you'll make it big in Hollywood."

"I want to be like you," Erin had said. "Will you teach me?"

Abby had beamed. "You bet I will!"

Erin had lots of time to study with her grandmother. Whenever her father, Marc, went on location to direct a film, Cassie went with him, often with an assignment from one of the magazines that featured her photo essays. The nannies and housekeepers in charge of Erin were only too happy to allow her to spend time with her grandmother.

When the part of Katie Norman, the middle sister on *The Family Next Door,* had come up, Abby had told Erin to go for it. By then Erin was twelve, and all she could think about or talk about was acting.

"You're exactly right for the part," Abby had said. "If you do a good job at the audition, it could be yours. Look through the photos your mother has taken of you. Pick out a good head shot. I'll help you put the rest of your résumé together and tell Zack he's got a new client, but don't count on any other help from me. You can do this on your own." She smiled, and her eyes glinted with mischief as she added, "What your agent might do for you is something else, of course."

Erin knew what Abby meant. Erin would have to be good, or she wouldn't be cast in the pilot. But if a choice had to be made among a number of talented girls, a director might be swayed, knowing there'd be plenty of free publicity for any show on which Abby Grant's granddaughter was making her debut.

Lots of actors in Hollywood had traded on their famous parents' or grandparents' names. It didn't bother them, and it wasn't going to bother Erin. She wanted to act more than she wanted anything else in the world, and intended to do her very best to win the audition, with or without help.

Her parents arrived home from location the week of the audition. That night at dinner, Erin had glanced at her tall, good-looking father, whose red hair and beard had always made her think of pirates. Just like a pirate, he sailed in and out of her life. Unfortunately, he always took the beautiful princess with him.

Among her earliest memories were the ones in which she'd stood with her hand clasped tightly by her nanny, watching her parents drive away in a taxi, headed for the airport.

"Smile!" her nanny would whisper. "You don't want to make your parents unhappy by giving them a crybaby face to remember."

And Erin, terrified she might make her parents so unhappy that they might not want to come back to her, would smile and wave until their taxi was out of sight. It was not until she'd been pulled inside and the front door had closed that she'd burst into loud sobs against her nanny's skirt.

Outsiders envied Cassie and Marc's closeness. "They're always together. They're the perfect, devoted couple," their friends raved.

*But they're not just a couple,* Erin wanted to shout. She wished she weren't the only one in her family who could count to three. But that wasn't what she wanted to think about now.

Erin took a deep breath for courage. "I want to audition," she said.

Cassie's fork dropped, clattering on her plate. "Audition? For what?"

"For a part in a TV pilot."

"A pilot? What kind of a program is it?"

"It's a situation comedy about an average American family."

Cassie groaned. "Where did you hear about this audition?"

Erin hesitated, trying to formulate an answer. Marc raised an eyebrow at Cassie and murmured, "Where do you think?"

Cassie frowned. "No matter what your grandmother may have told you, Erin, you aren't ready for this."

"I think I am."

"Only if Abby pulls a few strings."

Erin paused, but said truthfully, "Abby said she wouldn't help me. She said I'd have to do this on my own."

"But training . . . acting lessons . . ."

Erin didn't speak. Her parents looked at each other for a long moment.

"Of course, she's had lessons," Cassie said, and turned to look at Erin. "You've been studying with your grandmother, haven't you?"

Erin nodded.

"I should have known." Cassie's eyes were suddenly

damp with tears. "Erin's always been closer to Abby than she has to me."

Erin scrambled out of her chair and rushed to throw her arms around her beautiful mother, who still wore her hair long and unstyled, like a pale blond cloud around her face. "I love you, Mom," she said. "I love you so much, but Abby knows how I feel inside."

"Don't you think I do, too?"

Erin pulled back and studied her mother's face. "No. Not about this," she said honestly. "I don't think you do."

Cassie looked at Erin with bewilderment. "It's true that I can't understand your desire to work in television."

Erin bristled. "What's wrong with television?"

Cassie made an obvious effort to explain with patience. "Think about it, Erin. Your father's films have always been of such high quality. They've offered people something important, something worthwhile. In comparison, can't you see how shallow and superficial most situation comedies are?" She made "situation comedies" sound like "bubonic plague."

*They're rejecting just the kind of work Abby does.* Erin clenched her teeth and refused to answer.

Marc pushed back his chair, got up, and strode to Cassie's side. He took her hands, gently pulling her to her feet, and wrapped his arms around her. "Suppose we let Erin audition for the part," he said. "Any daughter of ours will quickly be able to see through the TV sham, and that will be the end of it."

"But what if she gets the part?" Cassie spoke to Marc as though Erin were not in the room.

"Don't worry about it," he answered. "There are always hundreds of kids after every part. If Abby's true to her word and won't pull strings, it's not too likely that Erin will be cast. She has no credits and no experience."

Erin tried to swallow the lump in her throat. Her parents stood together with Erin on the outside. They were sure that she'd lose the audition, took it for granted that she'd give up in defeat.

*I won't,* she thought. *I'm going to win that part. Abby knows, and I know, so it doesn't matter what anyone else thinks.*

And she *had* won it.

# 2

"*O*kay, cast. Let's get with it,"
John called. He headed back to the control room.

The first assistant director immediately yelled, "Quiet!"
and began the sequence of commands to the crew that
preceded the taping. The makeup artist swiftly powdered
noses as the hairdresser dashed onto the set and brushed a
stray curl away from Erin's forehead.

"Roll sound . . . Roll camera . . . Mark it!"

*Snap* went the slate in front of Erin's nose. The first line was hers. She erased everything from her mind but the scene she was going to play.

"Action!" Dave called out.

After the taping, the cast of *The Family Next Door* took over the dim, wood-paneled recesses of Roscoe and Ruby's. Someone turned the television to the channel carrying Abby's show as they all crowded into the red vinyl booths.

Erin found herself being roughly shoved into a corner. "Hey!" she complained, then looked up to see Eddie Jarvis grinning at her.

"Move over," he said. "C'mon, move, move."

Eddie was nothing like the nerdy character Clarence he played on the show. Erin had to admit that Eddie wasn't as handsome as guys like River Phoenix or Keanu Reeves or the Brat Pack actors like Emilio Estevez or his brother, Charlie Sheen, but there was a confident, honest smile in Eddie's eyes that intrigued Erin. He was so different from the other kids she knew who were actors. Their glances were constant appraisals; their conversations always had the slight edge of rivalry. Were your show's ratings higher than theirs? Did your photo appear in the latest issue of *People* magazine and theirs didn't? Did one of the columnists mention you as a possible for a film that was being cast? Erin hated to admit that sometimes she was guilty of this desperate, competitive thinking, too, but she was.

Eddie wasn't like that. He was easygoing, seeming to enjoy what he did each day without worrying about the next. His part on *The Family Next Door* wasn't enormous, but he worked as hard as anyone else. He was sharp, and Erin liked him a lot. She was glad they were good friends. If the competitive atmosphere on the set made it hard to have friends there, the way they worked made it impossible to find friends anywhere else.

Actors who had steady film or television jobs spent long hours every day on the set, and if they were under eighteen and hadn't passed the courses for high-school graduation, they crammed in the required hours of schooling set by the state of California. Each night, there was homework to do in addition to rewritten dialogue and blocking changes to memorize.

Erin had little in common with the few girls she knew who weren't in the business. They didn't understand her life, and she was bored with theirs. The couple of guys she'd dated for very short times couldn't seem to relax and forget that she was a star, so it was easy to forget them.

"If it isn't my nerdy boyfriend, Clarence," Erin murmured, scooting over to make room. "What are you doing here?" Eddie wasn't in that week's show, so he hadn't been at the taping.

"I called the set," he said. "They said you were running late, so I came on the chance I could find you. I wanted to watch Abby's show with you."

"Thanks," Erin said, and squeezed his hand.

Roscoe, the bald counterman, slapped a tray piled with hamburgers and fries on their table and stood back, scratching his stomach through a badly stained apron. "Anything else you folks want?" he asked, answering his own question by adding, "Ruby's bringing the soft drinks."

He suddenly caught sight of Eddie and grinned. "How's it goin', Clarence?"

"No problems," Eddie said. He pitched his voice higher, thrust his neck out, and blinked as though the lights were too bright, becoming Clarence Nutweilder. "How have you been, Mr. Roscoe?"

"Can't complain," Roscoe answered. He turned to Gene, one father to another. "At least you don't have to worry about Clarence, the way you have to worry over your oldest girl's boyfriends—like that Bill." He glanced around. "Where is Bill? And Andrea?"

"They had a date," Gene said, his face serious.

"Just keep an eye on 'em," Roscoe said, and waddled back toward the counter.

"He really believes we're the characters we play," Lydia said with a giggle.

"It just proves you're doing a good job," John said.

The drinks were brought to the table as a television network reporter came on with a news update.

"It's almost time," Gene said. He raised his voice to include those around them in the restaurant. "Quiet down, everyone. *The Abby Grant Show* is about to begin."

Most of the people in the diner were from the studio, but the few outsiders who'd wandered in stared at the cast of *The Family Next Door*. As a young woman caught Erin's eye, she shyly waved. Erin, who enjoyed being the center of attention and probably would have waved back at any other time, resented the intrusion and quickly turned her gaze to the television set.

She couldn't eat. She found it hard to breathe. She

held tightly to Eddie's hand as the sound was turned up and the lively theme music began. There was a quick sequence of shots of Abby from past films and her television series—a young Abby Grant in costumes of all types—mugging and grinning so outrageously that many of the people watching grinned back.

Erin had lied when she'd told Marcie that Abby didn't need a show. Her last situation comedy was a major flop. "Bad scripts," Abby had said. "The cast was good, but what could they do with stale jokes?"

Abby wouldn't give up. "Let's try a different format. We'll give them a variety show," she'd told the network brass. "There hasn't been a really good variety show in years. Not since Carol Burnett's."

When Abby's agent telephoned to tell her that network executives had agreed to a new pilot, Erin thought that her grandmother would be ecstatic. But Abby had put down the phone and slowly dropped into the nearest chair.

"Are you all right?" Erin had asked.

Abby had looked almost scared as she turned to Erin. "They'll give me a variety show, with a good-sized budget, too. If it gets good reviews and decent ratings, they'll schedule it in the fall as a regular, weekly show."

Erin had run to Abby, knelt in front of her chair, and clasped her hands. "Abby! That's wonderful news!" she'd shouted.

But Abby's hands were cold, and her voice was low and husky as she had asked, "Can I do it?"

Erin had sat back on her heels, amazed. "I've never

heard you say that," she blurted out. "Of course you can do it."

"It's an entirely new format. I'll have to start work with a dance coach. Oh, yes, a vocal coach, too. There'll be songs as well as skits." She had sat upright, the color coming back to her cheeks. "I've got to get in touch with Manny. He's the best comedy writer in the business."

Erin had grinned. "That's the way! Go for it!"

At Abby's insistence, none of the television critics would be allowed to see the taped show in advance, but some of the critics had expected the worst and had written negative predictions in their local or syndicated columns. They'd called Abby's brand of humor old-fashioned and out of style and predicted that her new show would be secondhand material in a fancy wrapper.

Now, in Roscoe and Ruby's, Erin watched the screen with a sick feeling in the pit of her stomach. She slowly became aware that the critics had been absolutely right.

Abby's "housewife" skit, in which she wore a frilly apron, a silk dress, and pearls, was ancient history. As Abby blinked from under a double row of artificial eyelashes, grinned, and sang off key through a layer of makeup as thick as house paint, Erin slumped against the booth in agony.

*The Abby Grant Show* wasn't just bad. It was a real bomb.

The enthusiastic laughter that came from the group surrounding Erin was as artificial as Abby's hair color.

*You don't have to laugh just to be nice to me!* Erin wanted to shout at them, but she realized she was being unreasonable. The Normans were a family, and this was what families were for, wasn't it? To stick together? To aid each other over the rough spots? The members of her television family were doing their best to help her, and Erin loved them even more for it.

The minute the show was over, she said, "I'm going to Abby's house. She's planning to celebrate there with a few friends." Somehow, she managed to smile thinly at the transparently pitiful comments her friends were making as she squeezed from the booth.

Erin's face grew warm, and she hoped that the rush of emotion that hurt so much wasn't pity. No one had the right to pity Abby Grant.

Any show—good or bad—was subject to cancellation. The end had come sooner or later for all Abby's shows. She'd handled it like a pro every time. Someday the end would come even to *The Family Next Door*. Erin wasn't sure she would have the same courage that Abby had shown in the past.

It wouldn't happen! America loved *The Family Next Door*. It couldn't happen! At least not for years. Erin shuddered and quickly pushed away the thought.

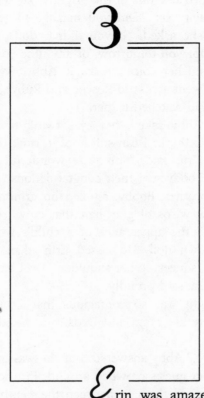

# 3

$\mathcal{E}$rin was amazed when she entered the den of Abby's large Beverly Hills home. She had dreaded walking into a group filled with gloom, but the wide glass doors were open to the floodlit garden and pool, and Abby and her guests were happily partying.

Abby put down her usual glass of club soda and held out her arms to Erin. The wide sleeves of her white chiffon gown floated out like wings and set off her burnished gold hair. She looked like one of the brightly painted angels in a primitive nativity set. "Did you manage to see the show, sweetheart?" she asked. "If you didn't, don't worry. We'll run the tape for you tomorrow, or any time you like."

Erin found her voice. "I saw it, Abby. So did most of our cast. We went across to Roscoe and Ruby's to get something to eat and watched it there."

"Well?" Abby asked, her eyes twinkling in pleasure. "What did you think? I can still hoof it, can't I?"

"Abby," Erin said, "you were wonderful. You always are. And everybody sent their congratulations."

Abby's brother, Bobby, ambled up grinning and nodding. The few wisps of gray hair that crowned his plump face gave him the appearance of a child's well-loved and well-worn clown doll. He kissed Erin, then put an arm around Abby, squeezing her shoulder. "Do I have a talented sis or what?" he said proudly.

His delight was so contagious that Erin grinned in return. "Where are Mom and Dad?" she asked. "I thought they'd be here."

"They are," Abby answered, but she was interrupted as a cluster of her guests crowded around. Erin knew most of them. She greeted them in between their enthusiastic burblings over Abby.

"She was wonderful!"

"Beautiful as ever!"

"The ratings are going to be super. Surely, Abby darling, they'll sign you for a weekly show."

Abby put on an exaggerated expression of horror. "Weekly? Could I physically take it week after week? Do you know how much hard work I had to put into this show?"

"Hard work?" Abby's lifelong friend, Mary Lou Robertson, gave Erin a hug, then turned back to Abby. "No one would guess it was hard work. That's where your talent comes in. The way your comedy flows, it all looks like second nature."

"Oh, *that* part," Abby said, throwing her arms wide in exaggeration. "I was talking about the rest of it, the sweeping up, scrubbing out the rest rooms, carrying coffee to the director. . . . Did I remember to tell you? It was a *very*-low-budget show."

Everyone laughed, and Abby let Mary Lou lead her past the plump white leather sofas to the buffet table that had been set up in front of the windows.

Erin glanced into Abby's living room, but her parents weren't among the guests in there. She walked through the house into the sun room, where her mother and father sat alone on one of the soft green loungers at the side of the indoor whirlpool tub.

It was quiet in the room, and Erin was grateful. She needed to figure out what had happened. She'd been so sure she'd have to try to console Abby, but Abby and her friends had liked the show. They'd actually liked it!

Erin plopped down on a nearby chair and said, "Did you get here in time to see Abby's show with her?"

Cassie's eyebrows drew together in a disapproving frown. "Don't say anything here, please," she said in a low voice. "We'll discuss it later."

Did her mother think she was a child who didn't know

how to behave? Indignantly, Erin said, "All I asked was if you saw the show."

Marc got to his feet. "I'm ready to call it a night." He held out a hand to Cassie, pulling her to her feet. "We've got an early flight tomorrow."

Cassie smiled at Erin, ignoring her outburst. "Why don't you come home, too? The three of us can sit around the kitchen table and have a cup of tea and talk. I'm going to miss you while we're away."

"Okay," Erin said, feeling even more out of sorts and thinking, *If you really missed me, you'd stay with me once in a while and not always go with Dad.*

As they said good-bye, Abby hugged Erin tightly, her eyes gleaming with excitement. Erin knew how Abby felt. She'd been there, too. It was as though you were sailing on wings made of praise and applause, high over the heads of everyone else. You were warm and golden and the most special person in the whole world, and nothing was as wonderful as that feeling while it lasted.

But what would happen to Abby's self-esteem tomorrow? The reviews would begin to come in. Newspapers and television first, magazine reviews over the next few weeks.

Erin thought about the hurt some critics could cause. She'd experienced it. Had she ever! When *The Family Next Door* had previewed, most of the reviews were complimentary, and some columnists had singled out Erin for a few words of praise. But two television critics had seemed influenced by the fact that Erin was Abby Grant's granddaughter and had made her pay for it—had made them both pay.

Erin would never forget those reviews. One critic had

written, "In some ways, Erin Jenkins's acting was reminiscent of the exaggerated posturing that has always been typical of grandmother Abby Grant's out-of-date comedy style."

There was another review that was impossible to forget: "Pretty little Erin Jenkins's role in *The Family Next Door* is an amusing bit of fluff, which seems to suit her. If she's like her grandmother, fluff is all she'll ever be capable of giving us. What are we in for? A family tradition of *Fluff, Son of Fluff, Fluff Rides Again?* Heaven help the viewing public!"

"Some of them can't resist the temptation to be cute," Abby had said as she'd taken the review from Erin's hands, crumpled it, and tossed it to the floor. "This critic is sure her readers will think she's clever."

"But she's *not.*"

"No," Abby'd told her. "At least her victims don't think so. You know that people are reading those reviews and maybe believing them, and you get a little sick and a little scared, and you wonder how many people she'll turn away who might have liked the show if they'd seen it. But you have to learn to be tough."

"Are you tough, Abby?"

"I hope so."

"Then reviews like that don't hurt you anymore?"

Abby had sighed. "Erin, sweetheart, they never stop hurting. They hurt like hell."

Erin was still thinking about that conversation as she pulled a chair up to the kitchen table and watched her mother search through one cupboard after another until she found the tea bags.

"There was no point in bothering Mrs. Hackett," Cassie said. "Besides, it's fun, the three of us in the kitchen making our own tea."

She poured boiling water into the pot, then settled in the chair next to Erin. "There," she said, looking pleased with herself. "Now you can tell us what you thought of Abby's show."

Erin was taken off guard. Both her parents were waiting, watching her. What did they want? "There isn't much to say about it," she murmured, "except . . . except it wasn't very good."

Her father nodded in agreement, and Erin relaxed. "I don't get it," she said. "The show was awful, but Abby and her friends all thought it was a big success."

Cassie poured three cups of tea. She put down the pot, leaned her elbows on the table, and turned to Erin. "Of course they thought the show was a success. There's a big difference in what Abby and her friends think of as entertainment and what others think."

"Mom, Abby's entertained people for years and years!" Erin protested. "It's just that this show turned out to be kind of . . . well . . . old-fashioned, I guess. That's what was wrong with it. Abby needed new writers, maybe a better director. The mistakes weren't her fault."

Cassie shrugged. "The show was her usual style of pratfall humor."

"You don't understand me!" Erin tried to lower her voice. This was not the time to lose her temper. Cassie and Marc would leave for location in the morning, and this should be a pleasant evening.

Marc reached for his cup of tea and held it as though he was using it to warm his hands. "Maybe you don't understand us," he said. "We were hoping you'd begun to develop some sound critical judgment."

"What is that supposed to mean?"

"It means that we've been expecting you to realize that real entertainment is not superficial. It has substance and depth and makes an impact on its audience."

Erin couldn't keep the light sarcasm from her voice. "In other words, if you're going to stoop to watching TV, then it's PBS or nothing."

Cassie sighed. "Don't you see that shallowness—a complete lack of purpose—was one of the reasons Abby's show wasn't funny?"

"No, I don't. Abby has always been able to make people laugh, and I can make people laugh, and that's a good thing, because people need some laughter in their lives." Erin pushed back her chair and stood. The faint orange-spice fragrance of the tea was enticing, but she couldn't stay in that room another minute. It was too difficult to hold back her temper and keep from blurting out things that later she'd wish she hadn't said.

"Well . . . yes, you're right, of course, about people needing laughter in their lives," Cassie said, "but a more classic form of humor—"

"Good night," Erin deliberately interrupted. "It's been a long day, and I need to get to bed." She paused. "And I want to be up in time to say good-bye before you leave."

"Good night, sweetheart," Marc said, but Cassie hesitated a moment before wishing Erin a good night, and Erin could see the disappointment in her mother's eyes.

*Why do you expect me to be just like you?* she thought unhappily as she turned away and walked toward the stairs. *I'm not, and I'm never going to be.*

In the morning, Erin pulled on a pair of jeans and a T-shirt and ran down the stairs to the entry hall, where her mother and father were making a last-minute check of their luggage.

Mrs. Hackett, their quiet, efficient housekeeper, with her gray-streaked hair pulled into a tight bun that was as unfashionable as her muted print dresses, stood to one side, ready to collect whatever might be remembered and needed.

"I know I've forgotten something," Cassie said. "Did I pack my blue blouse?"

Marc smiled at her tenderly and kissed the tip of her nose. "It doesn't matter. You look beautiful no matter what you're wearing."

As Cassie beamed at him, Erin shyly said, "Hi. Remember me?"

"Darling, I didn't see you there." Cassie smiled lovingly and opened her arms to Erin, who felt hot tears rush to her eyes as she held her mother tightly.

This time, Erin blurted her thoughts aloud. "I wish you wouldn't go," she mumbled against the Chanel fragrance of her mother's neck.

Cassie moved back a step, holding Erin's shoulders and studying her face with surprise. "Why, Erin," she said, "we'll be home in just three weeks, more or less, and you have your work at the studio to keep you busy."

Embarrassed, Erin shook her head, blinking away the tears. "I know," she said. "I guess I was being five years old again."

Her mother looked bewildered. "What do you mean, honey?"

Erin heard a car door slam and heavy footsteps on the drive. "Your taxi's here," she announced.

There was a rush of good-bye kisses as the luggage was carried to the taxi. Cassie rolled down the car window the moment she was inside and called, "Write to us!"

Marc leaned around Cassie, his cheek pressed against hers, and reminded Erin, "I left our address on my desk. You know how to get in touch with us if there's an emergency."

"We love you."

"Take care, Erin."

"We'll miss you, darling!"

As the taxi drove away, her parents turning and waving as they always did, Erin automatically waved in return. It wasn't until Mrs. Hackett moved to go back inside the house that Erin realized she was tightly clutching the woman's hand.

Erin realized that the reviews of Abby's new variety show were going to hurt when they began arriving. *But not too much,* Erin thought. *Please don't let them be too awful. This show meant more to Abby than she'd ever let on. At least, let some of the reviews be good.*

But none of them were.

By Monday evening, the reports on the low ratings for the show were in, and Abby had given up any pretense of trying to take the reviews in stride.

At a late dinner with Abby and Uncle Bobby, Erin

watched her grandmother poke at the food on her plate until she couldn't stand it any longer. She steered her to the comfortable sofa in front of the large-screen television in the den. The room was filled with congratulatory bowls and baskets of flowers, which were now beginning to wilt.

"These are my favorite," Erin said, touching the petals of one of the full blooms in the basket of dark-red roses that her parents had sent. She wished they were there. Maybe her mom would know what to do to help Abby cheer up.

Bobby ambled in, sat next to his sister, and held her hand. *If this happened to me, I wouldn't mope around and feel sorry for myself,* Erin thought impatiently. *Of course, I'd be unhappy, but I'd pick myself up and keep going.* She tried to imagine what it would be like to learn that her own show was over and she was out of a job, but the thought frightened her so much that she pushed it from her mind.

"Abby," she said, trying to sound cheerful, "forget the reviews. They're over. You can move on to something else." She went into a couple of hokey dance steps. "Why don't you and I learn a tap routine and take it on the road? Ta-da!"

"You're right about moving on to something else." Abby tried to smile. "That variety show was my long shot. My one chance to prove I still have what it takes. I didn't make it, so there's only one way to move on—go into another line of business. How do you think I'd make it as a used-car salesman?" She put on a cornball expression and babbled rapidly in a ridiculous country accent, "Yes, indeed, ladies and gents, I specialize. Boy, do I specialize! Used cars for used-up comics. Flat tires for flat ratings."

"Abby," Erin said, sitting beside her, "you know you have talent. Why does it matter what the television critics write?"

Abby spoke so softly that Erin could hardly hear her. "It matters."

"You knew you were taking a risk, going with a format the public wasn't used to. But you had the courage to do it. That's what's important."

Abby nodded. "You're right about it taking courage. It's the same for all actors. When you perform, you put your talent on the line. If the reviews aren't good, it's not just the show they're rejecting. Your talent makes the show. Your talent *is* the show. So they're rejecting *you* . . . you the actor, you the person."

"But that's not the way they mean it."

"Erin, sweetheart, I hope with all my heart you never get hit with a low blow like this," Abby said, "but there's no way you're going to understand how I feel unless it happens to you."

"I *do* understand," Erin protested. "Let's watch television," she suggested. Desperately, she punched the remote control, and a popular talk show came on. "You need a good laugh," she told her grandmother.

To Erin's horror, a plump young comic was saying, "And did you all see the Abby Grant variety show? I mean, didn't you think you'd gone back in time? All we needed was Beaver Cleaver, Lucy and Desi, and the cast from *Gilligan's Island.* . . . Three cosmetic companies fought over who'd get the contract for the stars' makeup. . . . And no, that wasn't L.A. smog you were looking through. It was the filters put on the cameras' lenses to take out the wrinkles. There were so many wrinkles left over that a couple of tourists thought the San Andreas Fault—"

"Shut up! Shut up! Shut up!" Erin yelled as she jabbed at the buttons, finally managing to turn off the television set. "Don't pay any attention to him, Abby," she said. "His jokes weren't jokes. They were stupid. Dumb. Nobody was laughing."

"Yes, they were," Abby said. "They thought he was funny."

Erin fought back the tears that pressed painfully against her eyes and blurted out, "It's not funny to be mean about someone! You've never done that, Abby!"

"But that's what's popular now," Abby said. "It seems that my humor is out of style."

Erin persisted. "You're wrong. Those stupid dorks who wrote that are wrong! There are a lot of people who'll watch the show faithfully and . . ."

"That's right," Bobby said, trying to look cheerful. "The critics have often made wrong calls. If the shows are popular with the people, they go on and on."

"There won't be a show," Abby said. Her voice was emotionless, like one dull, low note on an out-of-tune piano. "The ratings were lousy, and the reviews were deadly, so the network executives told me, 'People don't want variety shows.' My show is dead, and as far as I can see, so is my career."

Erin shivered. "Don't say that, Abby. I've never heard you talk like this. You've always been able to see the humor in everything. That's what you've taught me—laugh to keep from crying. You can't just give up."

"It's not giving up. It's facing facts. People have changed, and I haven't."

"Think of all your fans! They don't want you to change. You can count on them."

"Fans?" asked Abby. "You'd be surprised how fast they can forget. When I was very young . . ." She broke off and shook her head impatiently. "Never mind. Just believe me. I know. In this business, you can't count on anything."

Abby slowly stood up and kissed Erin on the cheek. "It's getting late, past my bedtime," she said. "I'll see you tomorrow, sweetheart."

"I'll walk upstairs with you," Bobby said. He puffed a little as he hoisted himself to his feet and held out a crooked elbow to Abby. "You want to branch out in a different direction? Well, I have an idea or two. This fellow I know is forming a group . . ."

Erin angrily tuned him out as they left the room. This wasn't the time to ask Abby for another loan. What Abby needed was a lot of strong moral support. Erin sighed. What was she going to do? What would Mom do if she were here?

Erin fumbled through her shoulder bag until she found the sheet of paper with the phone number of the motel where the cast and crew on her father's picture were staying.

The phone rang only twice before Cassie answered it, her voice fuzzy with sleep.

"Hi, Mom," Erin said. "It's just me—Erin."

"Erin?" Cassie seemed to grope with the word as though she'd heard a strange name and was trying to place it.

"Mom," Erin said, "I wish you'd come home."

"Why? What's the matter? Has something happened?" Erin could picture her mother sitting on the edge of the bed, eyes wide, completely awake now. Darn! She'd started all wrong. She hadn't meant to scare her mother.

"Yes and no. I mean, nobody got sick or broke an arm or anything. It's just that I'm worried about Abby. Her show got awful reviews, and she's depressed, and I don't know how to help her."

"Oh, dear." Cassie sighed. There was a pause before she added, "Better tell me what's been happening since we left."

So Erin went through the whole recital from the network reaction to the bad reviews, and even included the talk-show comic.

When she finished, Cassie said, "Well, this was a tough one, all right. Abby will hurt for a while, honey, and I ache for her, but she'll recover."

"Mom, you don't understand."

"Of course I understand," Cassie said. "She's my mother. I know her ups and downs better than you do."

"Mom," Erin said, fighting back tears of frustration as she tried to keep her voice under control, "I wouldn't have bothered you if I didn't think it was important."

She heard the catch in her mother's voice. "Bothered? Oh, Erin, please don't ever think you're bothering me."

"Well, I didn't exactly mean 'bothered,'" Erin stammered. This wasn't coming out right at all. She didn't want her mother to be upset. She wanted her to come home.

"Listen to me, honey," Cassie said, spacing her words patiently. "Your grandmother's a great actress. It's not just her work. It's her life. Drama is so much a part of her life that she can't separate the two. Right now she's been dealt a low blow, and she's not going to . . . well . . . suffer in silence."

"That's not fair!" Erin exclaimed. "I thought you'd be sympathetic!"

"I am sympathetic. Abby is my mother, and I love her, but I have to be realistic."

"What's real is that she's so depressed it scares me."

"How can I explain what I mean so you'll understand?"

"Not the way you've been doing it."

For a moment, there was silence. "Erin, don't be rude," Cassie said.

"Then don't say things like that about Abby."

Cassie's voice lost its patient tone. "Young lady, you're the one who insisted on getting into acting while you were still a child. Abby seems to have taught you everything except how to take the bad breaks, and believe me, there will be plenty of them! You'd better get used to it!"

"I should have known you'd get around to me," Erin muttered. "I called you because I thought Abby needed your help. I don't want to hear again why I shouldn't have an acting career."

"I don't know what I—"

Erin's voice rose until she was almost shouting. "You can help by coming home!"

Her mother didn't answer, and Erin could hear muffled sounds as though a hand had been placed over the receiver.

"Mom?" she asked. "Are you there? Mom?"

The voice that answered was her father's. Although he spoke slowly and calmly, his tone was as firm as it would have been during a problem on the set. "Take it easy, Erin," he said. "Apparently you've just succeeded in upsetting your mother and yourself. That doesn't accomplish anything, does it?"

"Dad," Erin said, "I don't need a lecture. I only called because I can't seem to help Abby, and I thought Mom could—if she'd just come home and try."

"I don't think you're listening to me," Marc answered. "That kind of attitude isn't getting you anywhere."

Erin took a deep breath. "Did Mom tell you what I said about Abby's show and how she's taking the bad news?"

"Enough of it so I can understand why you'd be unhappy."

"I'm glad you understand."

"I also agree with your mother," Marc said. "Abby's had setbacks before. Sometimes an argument with a director, a film project that's fallen through, whatever. You name it." Erin could hear the humor in her father's voice as he continued. "Whether she's ranted and raved or draped herself dramatically across a sofa, I've got to hand it to her. She's good. We can feel sorry for her and admire her performance at the same time."

Erin squeezed her eyes shut and groaned. "Dad, it's not like that this time."

"Sure it is. Just wait until her agent calls with an offer from Vegas or another TV spot. Abby will be up and at 'em, and you'll be wondering why you wasted so much time worrying about her. Trust me."

It was no use. Neither of them believed her. Neither wanted to listen. "Are you and Mom still planning to come home in three weeks?" Erin asked.

"We're right on schedule," Marc said. "We should be through filming by then, and if all continues to go well, we'll be back in L.A. by mid-March." He paused, his voice jovial. "You're not so good in the letter-writing department, honey."

"I'll try to write soon," Erin said. "Maybe tomorrow."

"How's the show going?"

"Okay. We'll be through taping for next season in less than two weeks." *And I'll miss my TV family. As much as I miss you and Mom,* she thought, feeling a pang of guilt at her disloyalty.

"We love you, Erin," Marc said.

"I love you, too," Erin said, and quickly hung up. She didn't want her father to know they'd been able to make her cry.

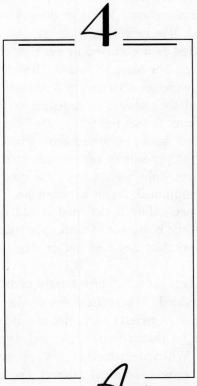

$\mathcal{A}$s she sat up and wiped her eyes, Erin realized that someone else had entered the room.

Uncle Bobby was sitting across from her, his cherubic face drooping with sympathy. "I heard some of your conversation," he told Erin. "I couldn't help it."

She shuddered as the last dry sob escaped. "I wanted Mom to come home to help Abby."

Bobby's hands fluttered as though they were trying to brush the problem away. "Cassie doesn't need to come home," he said. "I'm here to help Abby."

Erin flushed as it occurred to her that she might have hurt his feelings. She leaned forward. "Both Mom and Dad told me there were other times when Abby got upset about her career, and she's always managed to get through them with no problems. Is that right?"

"Of course," Bobby answered promptly.

Erin felt the pressure in her chest lighten.

"There have only been a few problems with her career," Bobby continued, "such as when her situation comedy was dropped. Abby understood it had run its course, but she didn't like being out of work. She didn't like feeling that the network had deserted her or that her fans didn't care."

"But her fans *did* care," Erin interrupted.

Bobby nodded. "There have been other downers for Abby. The divorces weren't easy. Her life didn't always run smoothly, but no matter what happened, I've always been there for her. When we were kids. When we were grown and your mother was just a kid. Always. I've always been at hand when she's needed me."

Erin's hope rapidly changed to doubt. She'd heard and seen enough about Uncle Bobby to know that he had it backwards. He hadn't always been there for Abby. Abby had been there for him. All through his life, happy-go-lucky, lovable Uncle Bobby had gone from one crazy scheme or investment to another, managing to scatter Abby's money in his wake. He still talked, now and then, about his life as a child star, forgetting he'd worked in only a few films, and as an extra at that.

Even now, with only a minor job in the publicity department of the Del-Lynn Studios in Burbank, Bobby referred to his "studio contacts" and to the "big money" he was going to make someday, but his older sister had provided all the comforts of life he'd enjoyed so far.

Bobby's forehead pleated into rows of wrinkles. "Just between you and me, Erin, I've never seen Abby get this depressed. Always before, she'd get angry. She'd talk about wringing necks and pounding down little pointed heads, and act out what she was going to do until we were both laughing, but this time it's different. She hasn't blown up. That's not like Abby, and I don't like it."

"What should we do?" Erin slumped in discouragement.

"I don't know," Bobby said. He hoisted himself from his chair and said, "Just be here for her. I guess that's the best thing. Is your show still taping? Will you be at the studio during the day?"

"Yes," Erin answered.

"Well, don't worry. I'll take some time off my job and get here early," Bobby told her.

"Uh . . . thanks," Erin mumbled.

As they walked to the front door, turning out lights on the way, Bobby smiled and said, "I never miss watching *The Family Next Door*, Erin, even the reruns. I'm awfully proud of you."

She paused and smiled back. "Thanks."

"You're so much like Abby was when she was young.

. . . Oh, not altogether in looks. I'm thinking about the drive, the ambition, the way the two of you put a career above everything else."

"Above everything else? Is that what I do? "

"I don't mean anything bad by that. I mean it in a good way. It shows that you know what you want out of life and you're not afraid to work hard for it. That's what made Abby great, and it's going to make you great, too."

Erin smiled again and gave a little shrug, not knowing quite how to answer.

Bobby hesitated, then said, "If anyone can reach through to Abby right now, it'll be you and not your mother. Cassie's a wonderful woman, but she and Abby—much as they love each other—have never been able to see eye-to-eye. As I said, I look at you, I see something of Abby. I look at Abby, I see something of you." He kissed her forehead, murmured good night, and left.

Erin leaned against the door. Bobby's words had distracted her. It *was* one of her goals, wasn't it? "I want to be just like you," she'd told her grandmother; now someone close to both of them had said, "You are."

Erin gazed up the broad sweep of stairs toward Abby's closed door at the head of the stairs and frowned. "But *I* wouldn't give up," Erin said.

Erin and Jake arrived at the entrance to the sound-stage at the same time. It was barely light, but the cool, still air was already yellowed and acid-sharp with the smell of smog.

"How's it goin', little babe?" Jake asked. He rested one

hand on her shoulder and the other on the handle to the heavy door.

"Fine," she said, and smiled up at him.

He smiled back, a slow, teasing smile. He didn't move toward the door, but stood there studying Erin, his hand holding her firmly in place.

*He knows how good-looking he is,* Erin thought, but she didn't care. Jake was intriguing. She liked his smile, and she even liked the way he was looking at her.

"You've been growing up," he said.

"That's the fate of child actors." She tried to sound sophisticated and hoped he couldn't tell how flustered he made her feel.

"And getting better and better looking. You like to party?"

"I guess. Sure." Erin couldn't tell Jake that she didn't go to many parties.

Jake let go of her shoulder. "Next time I hear about a good party, I'll keep you in mind," he said. "One of these days, I'll give you a call."

"Are you saying you're going to ask me out?"

He grinned. "Any reason why I shouldn't?"

"What about Marcie? I thought you and she—"

At that moment, Eddie stepped up behind her. "I've been sent here by the fire marshal," he said. "We've been getting complaints that you two have been blocking the door. Better move before we issue you a citation." He squeezed between them and tugged the door open.

Walking with Eddie, Erin followed Jake into the sound-stage.

"How's Abby?" Eddie asked. "Any better?"

Erin shook her head. "I wish she weren't so depressed. I called Mom. I wanted her to come home and see what she could do to cheer Abby. She said actors could expect ups and downs, and Abby would get over it—soon, even, if her agent called with a job offer." Her anger at her mother returned. "She refused to come home."

"Well, maybe she's right. She ought to know what her own mother is like."

Erin scowled at him. "Don't say that! It's practically what *she* said!"

"Okay, okay!" Eddie held up his hands protectively and pretended to duck.

Erin had to smile. "Very funny. When's the last time I threw a punch at you?"

"I just don't want you to start."

Erin glanced toward the set where Miss Blevins was waiting. "School time," she said. "I'll be glad when I can take my G.E.D."

"You've still got another year," Eddie said as they walked toward the cast and crew members, who were clustered in groups, some of them reading a trashy grocery-store tabloid.

"Don't remind me. July to March, and then I'll be free from school! Free forever!" She pretended to shudder and added, "Honestly, I can't imagine how anyone could stand to go to a regular high school six hours a day!"

Marcie turned from the group she was in and said, "You may find out what it's like."

"What are you talking about?" Erin asked.

"Haven't you read the new issue of *Snoop*?" She held up a copy of the newspaper. "There's an item in it about *The Family Next Door*."

Erin scoffed. "Big deal. Did a reporter for *Snoop* discover our head cameraman has a two-headed wife in Brazil? Or is the story about you? Did they finally find out you weren't human and had been cloned by aliens?"

Erin was surprised when Marcie didn't react to the dig with one of her usual superior smirks or a nasty crack. Instead, Marcie answered seriously, "According to *Snoop*, our show's over, and the Norman family will soon be history."

"That's crazy! We've got great ratings. We're always in the top ten."

"Read it." Marcie held out the newspaper and Erin grabbed for it, searching frantically until she saw the head for the story: *Norman Family to Split?*

She stared at the words, but for a moment she couldn't read them. The type swam in front of her, and her knees wobbled, and she groaned.

"Erin?" she heard Eddie ask from far away. She struggled to bring herself to the present.

"I'm all right," Erin said. She managed to read the short newspaper item. When she finished, she shoved the newspaper in Eddie's direction and complained, "That story is nothing but garbage. It didn't say anything. All it amounts to is just a stupid rumor that the network doesn't have *The Family Next Door* scheduled in its lineup for next fall."

She looked for reassurance to John, who was standing

nearby, frowning as he checked the shooting script for the next scene to be shot. "It *is* just a rumor, isn't it, John?"

"Who knows where a rag like that gets its information?" he answered. He stretched to look over the heads of those in the group behind him and ordered, "Sherri, I need to talk to you about this kitchen scene."

Jake ambled up. "Could be a leak." He shrugged. "Maybe somebody in one of the network offices tipped a reporter."

"Then that would mean the story is true!"

"Don't worry about it," Eddie reassured Erin. "You pointed it out yourself—the story doesn't really say anything. It's about as truthful as anything else in *Snoop*."

As John barked an order at one of the grips, Tina stepped up and took Erin's hand. "John acts mad. Is he mad at us?" she asked.

Erin, her mind on the story, pulled her hand away and gave Tina an absentminded pat on the shoulder. "He isn't mad at anyone," she said. "He probably doesn't like the news story any better than the rest of us do."

Still shaken, Erin walked over to join Lydia and Gene, who had moved some of the canvas director's chairs a little apart from the others to do a quick run-through of their lines.

Gene smiled as Erin approached. Lydia quickly asked, "Erin, dear, how's Abby holding up?"

She should have known that Lydia was kind and loving enough to worry about someone else instead of that dumb rumor in *Snoop*. Gratefully, Erin answered, "She's taking the reviews pretty hard. I'd like to help her, but I don't know what to do."

"Sit down and tell us about it," Lydia said. She picked up a script, her handbag, and a novel that she'd piled on a nearby canvas chair and moved them out of the way. Erin caught a glimpse of the novel. *The Dorchesters*. The story Marcie wanted a part in. She leaned over to study the book jacket.

Lydia put the book on Erin's lap. "If you'd like to read this, I'll let you borrow it. It's a great story, but keep a box of tissues on hand."

"Thanks," Erin said.

"Now, tell us about Abby."

Erin looked from Lydia to Gene. "Abby was terribly hurt by the reviews her show got." She went on to report Abby's reaction.

When she'd finished, Lydia murmured, "Poor darling. She needs a lot of tender, loving care."

"I can understand how Abby feels," Gene said, "and I'm sure Lydia's had moments like that, too. I think it's to be expected in this business. I guess what I'm saying is that we all get depressed, and we all get over it."

Lydia leaned back and smiled at Erin. "Abby is having a bad time now, but she'll work through it," she said. "It will just take time and patience."

"If her agent calls with another job, that will help more than anything else," Gene added.

"Of course it will." Lydia smiled tenderly at Erin.

Erin shifted on the canvas chair and relaxed. Finally, someone besides her understood how rotten Abby felt. And

Gene and Lydia were right. Abby was a pro. She'd bounce back in time. "You guys are wonderful," Erin said. "Thank you."

Lydia giggled and looked modest, while Gene smiled broadly.

"I mean, you really try to understand," Erin said. "You're just the way parents should be."

Someone on the set yelled, "Ten minutes!" The three of them, used to obeying studio rules, automatically got to their feet.

That evening, as they left the studio, Erin told Eddie about her conversation with Gene and Lydia.

"It sounds a lot like what you said your parents told you," Eddie said.

"No!" Erin protested. "It wasn't the same thing at all. Lydia and Gene were sympathetic about Abby. They weren't like my parents. Mom and Dad . . . well, they have an attitude."

"What kind of attitude?"

"C'mon. You know what I mean. It's like they think they're the only two people in the world and don't know anybody else is alive."

" 'Anybody,' meaning you?"

"You don't understand," Erin said.

Eddie gave her a tentative smile. "O wise and power-ful one, you think *I'm* the one who doesn't understand?"

She had to smile back. "Of course you are. It couldn't be me."

"Good. You're beginning to sound more like yourself," he told her.

As they walked out to the parking lot, Marcie hurried up to them, stopping next to Erin to thrust a folded newspaper at her.

"What's this?" Erin asked. She tried to seem nonchalant, but was suddenly a little frightened. "Not more about that rumor in *Snoop*?"

Marcie shook her head. "No, this isn't a rumor. This is a legitimate newspaper that deals in real facts."

Erin glanced at the paper, which was folded open to a review of Abby's show. Erin had read this review. It had been particularly negative and was one that had hit Abby hard.

Marcie grinned broadly as she said, "I thought you'd like to have this for your scrapbook."

"How do you do that?" Erin asked as she stared intently at Marcie.

Marcie looked puzzled. "Do what?"

"Talk without moving your lips. It's sort of cute, in a way, like Miss Piggy. Is it hard to do?"

Marcie mumbled something rude and pushed past Erin, hurrying across the parking lot.

"Now, that's more like it," Eddie told Erin. "What I said must have been worth something. You really are getting back to normal."

Erin smiled as she swatted at him with the newspaper.

Eddie took it from her hands and dropped it into the nearest trash can. "There," he said. "See how easily you can get rid of your problems?"

That's where he was wrong, Erin knew. Her problems with her parents and with Abby—who'd always helped Erin but who now needed help Erin didn't know how to give—wouldn't disappear that easily. And neither would the nagging feeling that there might be a scrap of truth behind the *Snoop* story.

Erin tried to push the worry away by telling herself firmly, *I asked John, and he said it was just a rumor.* But as the conversation with John suddenly and vividly replayed itself in her mind, Erin had to admit to herself that John hadn't really answered her question.

5

*7*he next day, the rehearsal went smoothly. Buoyed by the good spirits of everyone else on the show, who obviously weren't concerned about that item in *Snoop,* Erin ran to one of the pay phones at a midafternoon break and telephoned Zack Fremont.

Zack's father, Norm, had been Abby's agent from the time she was in her teens. Zack had always been Erin's agent, and he had become Abby's agent, too, when Norm retired. Zack was successful—maybe even a little more than his father had been—but conversations with Zack were always rushed. Even when Zack was the bearer of good news, Erin could picture him shifting the telephone receiver from ear to ear, staring at his watch, and drumming his fingers on his desk.

As she dialed Zack's office number, Erin doubted she'd be able to reach him right away. To her surprise, Zack's secretary put her through. It *was* a good day. Everything was working out.

"I'm not calling about myself," Erin said as soon as the greetings were out of the way. "I'm calling about Abby."

There was a moment of silence before Zack said, "That's a real shame about Abby's variety show. I think the network biggies made a mistake. Myself, I would have spent a few more bucks to make some changes, pick up the tempo, get some younger, fresher faces in the act. You know."

At least he hadn't blamed Abby. "Zack," Erin said, "Abby's taking it pretty hard."

His voice was so thick with sympathy that it dropped in tone. "Yeah. That's bad. Real bad. But those are the breaks." His words suddenly picked up speed, as though the sympathy was over and done with and now it was time to move along. "Look, I'd like to talk, but I've got to leave for a meeting in a few minutes—"

Erin interrupted. "I won't keep you. I only want to ask if you know of anything that might work out for Abby. The sooner she can get back to work, the better."

"Right off the top of my head . . . no."

"I read about the Santa Monica dinner theater that's

going to be doing that crazy parody of *Casablanca*. If they haven't cast it yet, what about Abby for the Ingrid Bergman role?"

"Erin, baby, get real. Abby is at least thirty years too old for that part."

Erin sighed. "Can you line up something for her in Vegas?"

"She was there just last year. They want variety, not the same old faces." Zack shifted gears again and added, "Got to run, Erin, but I promise I'll keep it in mind. Something will come up."

"Zack, it would really mean a lot to Abby."

"I said *I promise,* baby, and I keep my word."

"That's right. You do," Erin admitted, beginning to feel hopeful again.

As she walked back to the set, Tina ran to meet her.

"I want to go to the zoo," Tina said, "but Mama says I can't. Last time, people pushed me and wanted me to sign their autographs. They scared me, and I cried."

Erin nodded. "Those people are fans. They're the ones who keep us working, but it's tough when we want to go anyplace in public."

Tina swung on Erin's arm as they continued on their way to the set. "Aren't I ever going to go to the zoo?" she asked.

"Maybe if you went in disguise," Erin said, amused by the obvious crush Tina had on her. "You could wear a thick black mustache and pull a big hat over your eyes." She stopped and dramatically slapped a hand to her forehead.

"No! That won't work. What if you accidentally ate your mustache with your popcorn?"

Tina squealed with delight. "Or my mustache got stuck in my ice-cream cone!"

"I'll just have to think of another disguise." Erin bent to whisper. "You could wear a brown paper hump and spit at people, and they'd think you were a camel."

"They'd put me in a cage!" Tina shrieked, jumping up and down.

"Wouldn't you like that?"

"No!"

"Then, what if you . . ."

"Tina! Stop screaming!" Marcie appeared in front of them, hands on hips, legs apart. "You're making so much noise, you're giving me a headache."

Tina shrank against Erin's legs.

"She's just a child," Erin said. "Pick on someone your own size."

Marcie smirked. "Well, that lets you out, too, doesn't it?"

"Don't mind her," Erin said to Tina as Marcie flounced back into the area of *The Family Next Door* set. "There's your mother. She's waiting for you."

Tina tugged on Erin's skirt. "I have to tell you a secret," she said.

Erin obediently bent down, and Tina whispered, "A reporter from a magazine interviewed me. She asked me who I liked best in *The Family Next Door,* and I said you. I told her you were the nicest. You weren't my pretend sister. You were my real sister."

"That's sweet," Erin began, realizing she should say something to set Tina straight but not knowing how to do it.

But Tina wasn't listening. "My mommie told me that I shouldn't say things that weren't nice about anybody, but Mommie went in the kitchen to make some iced tea, and I told the reporter that I didn't like Marcie at all." She put her fingers over her mouth, trying to smother the laughter.

"You and me both, sweetie pie," Erin said. Who was she to try to explain the difference between real family and pretend family to Tina, when her own feelings were every bit as mixed up?

Abby, Bobby, and Mrs. Jefferson, Abby's middle-aged housekeeper, were waiting for Erin to join them for dinner when she got to Abby's that evening. Erin dropped her purse and *The Dorchesters* on a table in the den and hurried to the dining room, slipping into the one vacant place.

When Erin had been very young and used to the rules in her own home, she'd asked Abby why her housekeeper ate dinner with her. "Is it so you don't have to eat dinner by yourself if I'm not here?"

Abby had smiled and said, "Mrs. Jefferson and I are friends. It's nice to eat dinner sometimes with a friend, don't you think?"

It had made perfect sense to Erin, as did anything Abby chose to do.

Dolores, the slender, shy young woman who cooked for Abby, placed a filled plate in front of Erin. It contained a small beef fillet, an even smaller baked potato, a sliced tomato, and lots of broccoli. Erin decided that Mrs. Jefferson must be dieting again. As soon as they had all been served and Abby had lifted her fork, Erin hungrily attacked her food.

Uncle Bobby's voice was overloud and overcheerful. "How is the taping going?" he asked Erin.

"Fine," she said. She glanced at Abby from the corners of her eyes. Her grandmother was methodically eating her broccoli spears as if she were trying to get rid of them.

"Any word yet on renewal of the show?" Bobby asked.

In surprise, Erin shifted her attention to Bobby. "Why do you ask that? It'll be renewed. There's no question about it. The ratings are still high."

"Will you finish according to schedule?"

"I think so."

Bobby smiled. "Then you'll get a well-needed vacation."

"I don't think of it as a vacation," Erin said. "I love doing the show, and when we're not working I miss everyone. It's like having another family and not seeing much of them until we start taping again in the fall."

Abby looked up, her interest finally caught. "I know what you mean," she said. "When the entire cast is working well together, it gives the show a good feeling. And the audience picks up on it."

"I really miss Lydia and Gene during the summer months," Erin admitted. "Oh, I know we go to John's beach house in Malibu a couple of times for cookouts, and everyone's there. And Lydia always has us all to dinner. But it's like having your parents go on a long vacation and having to do without them instead of living in the same house with them."

"You should be used to parents like that," Abby said dryly.

Bobby looked up, surprised, Mrs. Jefferson's dark eyes widened, and Erin could feel her face grow warm.

"Cut," Abby said, drawing the side of her hand across her throat. "Strike that line. I have no right to take out my bad mood on other people."

"It's okay," Erin said. "It's the truth."

"Your parents love you very much," Abby told her, "and I'm behaving like the Wicked Witch of the West."

The phone rang, and they were all silent as Mrs. Jefferson got up from the table and answered it in the sun room.

She appeared again in the doorway and said to Abby, "It's for you, Miss Grant. It's Mr. Fremont."

Erin heard Abby suck in her breath. "I wonder what Zack wants. It's late for a business call."

"The only way you'll find out is to talk to him, Abby." Erin said. "Who knows? Maybe it's a job." She found she was gripping the edge of the table so hard that her knuckles hurt.

Abby slowly pushed back her chair, rose gracefully, and strolled into the sun room.

Erin let out the breath she was holding and whispered, "I hope, I hope, I hope."

Bobby's face was alight with eagerness. "Do you think the network people changed their minds? Will there be a show after all?"

"No," Erin said abruptly, annoyed by his impractical wishful thinking. "But it could be another job, something just as good."

Abby was back in a few moments. Without saying anything, she sat down and picked up her fork. Erin leaned toward her grandmother. Did she look different? Happier? Erin couldn't tell. "What did Zack say?" she asked.

"Nothing much," Abby answered. She cut a small piece from her steak. "There's a big benefit performance for the March of Dimes being planned in Houston, and apparently the socialite who's chairperson of this fund-raiser practically begged Zack to get me there." Abby looked down modestly, but her cheeks grew pink. "She went so far as to say she wants this to be the most successful fund-raiser Houston has ever seen, and it won't reach the top without me."

"What routine will you do?" Erin asked. "What will you wear? Will the show be televised?"

Abby laughed, and Erin was so glad to hear that laugh that she wanted to jump up and hug her grandmother.

"I don't know the answers to any of those questions. Zack is going to call back," Abby said. "He didn't have much information to go on. First he wanted to find out if I'd do it."

"You said you would, didn't you?"

"It wasn't hard to talk me into it," Abby said. "I'm always a sucker for a good charity." Abby began to tackle her dinner with vigor. "The Wicked Witch of the West seems to have vanished. Who's got the ruby slippers?"

The telephone rang again, and Abby jumped up, saying, "I'll get it. Zack said he'd call right back."

With a grin, Bobby said, "It's going to be like old times again." He turned to Mrs. Jefferson. "I'm still hungry. What's for dessert?"

"No dessert," she said. "We could all stand to lose a few pounds."

"Not tonight," Bobby said firmly. "This is a time for celebrating. If there's any more of that chocolate ice cream, or . . ."

He stopped speaking as Abby entered the room again, her shoulders bent with discouragement. She plopped into her chair, slumping, and let out a sigh.

Erin stared. "What's the matter? What happened?"

"The Houston gig wasn't exactly what we thought it was."

"You mean it's not a benefit performance?"

"Benefit, yes. Performance, no."

"I don't get it," Bobby said.

"It's a format they've used successfully for the past few years for the March of Dimes. They have a ballroom set up with elaborately decorated kitchens manned by some local celebrities and socialites, with a few national personalities tossed in for good measure. People buy tickets and visit the various kitchens, sampling the recipes. My hostess was supposed to be teamed with a TV news anchor, but the anchor drifted to Boston, and the hostess was left stranded. Since the event is next week, she went into a state of panic. Then she remembered that she'd met Zack at somebody's Hollywood party and gave him a call."

"But she asked for you specifically," Erin insisted, trying to salvage the situation.

"So Zack says, but I doubt it."

"Abby, she'd be thrilled to get you to come! You know she would!"

Mrs. Jefferson plunged into the immediate problem. "Maybe I could find you a recipe that isn't too difficult," she said, "and I'll have to lend you an apron. I know for sure you don't even own one."

Abby shook her head. "Don't worry about that part. The aprons and costumes are taken care of. So is whatever it is we're going to cook. My hostess has a chef lined up who'll do the basics. All we have to do is stir the pot, smile at the people, and make a show of having a good time."

"Oh, Abby," Erin said, "I hope you'll go. You'll have fun, and think how thrilled they'll all be. The reason they hadn't asked you in the first place is that they wouldn't have dared. You're a bigger star than they could hope for."

"Past her prime."

"No!" Erin began, but Abby didn't let her interrupt.

"Don't worry. I accepted. I'll go to Houston and look cute in my costume and stir the pot of soup or whatever it is. I'll smile, I'll twinkle, I'll be a good little drawing card." Abby sighed and said, "I know how to do it. I've been there before. The audience wants to look, to stare, to tell their friends, 'Guess who I saw!' " She began to hum, then sing in a high-pitched voice, "I'm a little cookie, cookie, cookie . . ."

Erin knew that song. She'd heard it when she'd run the tapes of the movies her grandmother had made as a very little girl. But now she was puzzled, even a little fearful at Abby's strange behavior. "Why are you singing that song, Abby?" she asked.

Abby stopped and shook her head. "Wrong line," she said. "You're supposed to ask, 'Didn't you used to be Cookie Baynes?' Or maybe now they'll ask, 'Didn't you used to be Abby Grant?' "

Erin felt cold all over. Unthinking fans had asked that question of more than one actor who'd been out of the limelight. Her thoughts raced back to that awful story in *Snoop*.

She could see bulging eyes and hear a voice rasping in her head: *Didn't you used to be Erin Jenkins?*

"No!" she cried, half rising from her seat and facing her startled grandmother. "Don't say that, Abby, because it's not going to happen!"

6

$\mathcal{D}$ressed only in one of the
overlarge T-shirts she wore to sleep in, Erin lay across her
own bed in her parents' large hillside home, script in hand.
She knew she should be studying the lines that had been
rewritten, but she couldn't keep her mind on the script.

It wasn't her grandmother's problems that were preoc-
cupying Erin now. Abby's trip to Houston had gone well.
She'd been treated royally, which helped her injured ego,

and even though Abby still tended to mourn her lost variety show, her sense of humor had begun to come back.

Tomorrow would be the last day of taping for *The Family Next Door*, and on Saturday John would give his annual wrap party for the cast and crew. No one had spoken about the *Snoop* article in days, and Erin felt a little silly about the way she had reacted to it.

She was still in a strange mood, but for a more ordinary reason. A wrap party always brought out mixed emotions in her. There was the feeling of pride in what a season's hard work had accomplished, but there was also a sense of loss. The members of her make-believe family would be going their separate ways, and she'd see them infrequently until they came together again in July.

Some of them would work just as hard from March until July as they did the rest of the year. Lydia loved theater, and for the past two years had starred in local productions. Last summer, Erin had gone to see Lydia's play at the Mark Taper Forum, and found herself in awe of her "mother's" dynamic performance. Erin had had no idea, judging only from the quiet, typical-mother role Lydia played on *The Family Next Door*, that Lydia had such a breathtaking talent. Her TV role as Nancy Norman, which had made her famous all across the United States, certainly didn't do her justice.

Gene was a popular character actor who always had a film role to walk into. Marcie had moved up last year into big box office when she'd starred as a teen prostitute in a film that had received wide acclaim. There had even been talk for a while that Marcie might receive an Oscar nomination. Erin had felt a moment of sheer joy when the list of nominees was announced and Marcie wasn't on it.

Erin wished that she could be cast in a meaty role like that. Pug-nosed Erin Jenkins as a street-walking runaway—right. She laughed aloud.

Back to the script. Tomorrow had to go perfectly. The next day was the wrap party, on Monday and Tuesday were end-of-the-school-year exams, and later next week—if all went according to schedule—Mom and Dad would be home. Erin tried to concentrate on her lines, but it was awfully hard.

The next morning, Tina was the first to greet Erin as she stepped inside the big soundstage and bounced next to Erin on the way to the set. "Tomorrow's the party," she said. "At John's beach house. I wish we could go swimming. Don't you?"

Erin pretended to shiver. "Not in this weather. The water's too cold."

"Mommie said pretty soon I'll be making two commercials. One's for hot dogs. I like hot dogs, so that's a good one."

"What's the other one?"

"I don't remember. Soup, I think."

*Everybody's got something to work on except me.* Erin wished that Tina's mother would call her, but Tina stuck to her side, still chattering. "Mommie said we won't be working on the show for four months," Tina said.

"That's right."

A touch of sorrow crept into her voice. "I'll miss you. Will you come and see me, Erin?"

Erin stopped in surprise and looked down at the child. "Of course I will," she said. "You've been on the show for two years, and both summers I came to see you, didn't I?"

"Not very often."

"As often as I could. You were working, and so was I." Speaking to herself, Erin grumbled, "At least I had a couple of commercials to do."

Tina made a grab for Erin's hand and clung to it. "Let's go to Disneyland," she said, a mischievous smile lighting her face. "Could you make us some disguises so nobody would know us and we could go to Disneyland?"

Mrs. Reed's voice rang out. "Tina!"

"Mommie wants me," Tina said.

Mrs. Reed stood at the edge of the set and waited until Tina came to her. Then she took the child's hand and led her down the hall toward the schoolroom.

"At least my mother doesn't treat me like a puppy," Erin mumbled.

"Talking to yourself?"

Erin whirled to see Eddie, who had come up behind her. "I was just thinking about Tina's mother," she said.

"She's not so bad," Eddie said, "not as bad as some mothers."

Erin gave him a searching look. "I've never met your mother."

"That makes us even."

"But I've told you about mine, and you've never said a word about your mother."

"Let's leave it like that. Want me to walk you to the schoolroom?"

"Sure," Erin said. "If you want to."

"I want to. In fact," Eddie added, "I'd like to take you out tonight."

"You mean a date?"

"No, I mean a business meeting. I'd like to discuss contracts and investments."

Erin laughed. "Okay. I admit it was a stupid question. I just . . . well, it took me by surprise."

"We're good friends, aren't we?"

"Yes," she said. "Very good friends."

"Isn't it okay to date a very good friend?"

"I don't know," Erin said. "What if we go out together for a while, and things change for one of us, and we stop being good friends?"

"And what if we get picked up by a UFO, and my hair falls out, and your nose turns blue? Look, Erin, I thought we could drive down Beverly Boulevard to Pacifica and get something to eat. Is there anything wrong with that?"

"No," she said. "I've never been there, and I'd like to go. I'll have to call Mrs. Hackett and tell her I'll be home late."

"Any problems with that?"

"I guess not. She'll just want to know where I am."

"Tell her I'll follow you home, so you can leave your car. Seeing my honest face will put her at ease." He smiled and went into his Clarence voice and pose. "Adults don't worry about the Clarences of this world."

As they passed the door to the makeup room, Jake strode through, doing a quick sidestep to keep from bumping into Erin.

"Hi, Erin," he said. He kept his eyes on her as he nodded in Eddie's direction.

"Hi," she answered.

"My big scene's coming up," Jake said, and Erin could hear pleasure warming his voice. "They gave me some good lines, so there's lots of tension, you know? Although it's kind of hard to believe . . . I ask Andrea to go away with me for the weekend, and she turns me down." He grinned and flexed his muscles. "Now, if it was Clarence here—"

"If it was Clarence," Erin interrupted, "she might have considered the invitation."

She brushed past Jake and hurried down the hall to the small schoolroom. Miss Blevins and Tina sat at two of the four desks. Tina's mother had settled herself into a chair next to Tina's desk and was already busy knitting. Marcie, of course, was on the set with Jake and would work in her study time later.

Eddie followed Erin as far as the doorway and grinned as he said, "Thanks for the endorsement. I'll keep it in mind."

"I was talking about Andrea Norman," Erin said, "not myself."

"And about Clarence Nutweilder and not me?"

Erin stopped and studied him. "Sometimes I get mixed up about how much is you and how much is Clarence. We've known each other over a year, but there's a lot I don't know about you, Eddie."

"Then that's wrong," he said. "Good friends should know about each other. We'll have to take care of that."

As he stopped speaking and looked into her eyes, Erin

suspected that Eddie wanted them to be more than just good friends. She took a quick breath, wondering just exactly what it was *she* wanted.

It was late when John called it a wrap, and even later when the cast and crew finally left the soundstage. *The last day of taping is always like this,* Erin thought. *No one wants to believe we've come to the end.*

But it wasn't really the end, Erin reminded herself. They'd be together as a family once again in July.

In her dressing room, Erin packed into a small travel case the few personal things left there and met Eddie back on the set.

"See you tomorrow," people were calling to each other. The wrap party at John Haywood's house would be cast and crew together. John always included everyone who worked on the show.

Eddie put an arm around Erin's shoulders and guided her out the soundstage door and across the lot to the parking area, where Erin's red Mercedes was parked near Eddie's ancient and dented humpbacked VW. She'd had to argue for weeks to talk her parents into letting her buy her own car, but she'd won. She loved her Mercedes, because it was a symbol of the career she'd earned for herself.

"I'll follow you home," Eddie said.

"I'll give you directions."

"I don't need directions. Your house is up above Sunset in Bel-Air, isn't it? I saw a picture of it in *Los Angeles* magazine."

"Okay," Erin said with a smile. "Let's get going. I'm hungry."

They had missed the worst of the rush-hour traffic, but the drive still took almost an hour. Erin turned the radio up to hear a Tracy Chapman song. In spite of being tired and hungry, she found she was happily anticipating her date with Eddie. Was he right? Was it true that good friends could date without its ruining their friendship? *What if he begins to like me too much, but I don't feel that way about him?* she thought, then felt a shiver run up her backbone as the next question popped into her mind: *What if I start feeling romantic about him, and he doesn't care?*

Erin had never been in love. She'd had quick crushes on some of the men she'd worked with, and last year she'd been totally and secretly infatuated with a muscular guy who worked for a while as a lighting grip on the set. Love hadn't seemed important so far. And there was no reason why it should be—not for a few more years, at least.

It took only minutes to carry her things inside, run a comb through her hair, and introduce Eddie to Mrs. Hackett. A couple of letters for Erin were lying on the hall table, and she could see her mother's familiar handwriting on one of them. She reached for the letter, then hesitated. *She's probably written to complain that I haven't been writing to them often enough.* She'd have plenty of time to read that later.

Erin took Eddie's hand and led him out the door. "I'm starving to death," she said. "Let's go."

Eddie's car had a few strange rattles, and the handle to the window on the passenger's side was broken. Erin sat on a lump in the seat where a spring had come loose, so to avoid it she moved to the middle of the front seat, close to Eddie.

"Sorry about the state of this old clunk," he told Erin as they took the road downhill, heading for Sunset. "I've saved up just about enough for the car I want, and now that the taping is over, I'll have time to go car shopping."

"What kind of car? BMW? Porsche?" she asked.

"Nope," he said. "Bronco. With all-terrain tires."

Erin gave an uncertain laugh "All-terrain?" she said. "There's just one kind of terrain in this town, and it's all under development."

He grinned. "The only way to live in this megalopolis is to be able to get out of it."

"If you want that kind of a car, why don't you get a Range Rover?" she asked. "That's the hot car to have."

"People in Beverly Hills who drive Range Rovers rarely go beyond Rodeo Drive," Eddie scoffed. "A Ford's good enough to take me where I want to go."

"Where is that?" Erin asked.

"To the quiet places. Like the mountains. Do you know it's so quiet there you can hear the pines murmuring? It's sort of like they're talking to each other."

He glanced at Erin, suddenly a little shy, as though he thought she might laugh. When she merely nodded, he continued. "I like the ocean, too. I like to walk along the beach just close enough to the waves so that the foam hisses up between my toes and seems to whisper. Do you like to do that?"

"I don't know," Erin said. "I think I would."

"What do you mean, you think you would? You've been to the beach and the mountains, haven't you?"

"Yes," Erin said, "but there have always been people

around. Maybe I should have yelled for everyone to be quiet, and then I would have heard what you've heard."

Eddie was silent for a moment, guiding the car into the fast-moving traffic, and she said, "You really weren't kidding me about the Bronco, were you?"

"What makes you think I was kidding?" He swung to glance at her with surprise before returning his attention to the street.

"Well, a Bronco's not a Beverly Hills kind of car," Erin said.

"Not everybody lives in Beverly Hills."

"But isn't that what you want?" She shrugged impatiently. "You know what I mean. It could be the Valley, or Malibu Colony, or Bel-Air. It doesn't matter what you call it, it's the Beverly Hills lifestyle. It's what every actor wants— the proof that he's made it."

"Is that what you want, Erin?"

She grinned. "You know it. Isn't that what we all want as soon as possible—success and recognition? I started working for it at a young age. And you started even younger. Isn't that right?"

It was hard for Erin to hear Eddie, he spoke so softly. "It was what my mother wanted. I'm not sure if I do or not."

She gave him a quick glance. "I thought you didn't want to talk about your mother."

He kept his eyes on the traffic, but he said, "I also told you that best friends should know about each other. I guess that's part of knowing about me. I don't get along with my mother at all. I moved out of the house she bought with my money as soon as I legally could."

Erin didn't speak, and Eddie finally said, "I was never a child to her. I was a money-maker. The only problem was, whatever I did wasn't enough. I wasn't famous enough or rich enough. There was always some other kid my age who did it better."

"I'm sorry," Erin said. She reached up and took his right hand from the wheel, for a moment holding it against her cheek.

He looked at her and smiled. "So now you know. I haven't got any other secrets. My life's pretty uncomplicated."

Erin smiled back encouragingly. "You like to act, don't you?"

"I like it."

"Then I don't understand what's bothering you about it."

"I keep thinking about the disadvantages that go with being an actor." Eddie took a sharp left turn onto a street lit with garish neon signs, and Erin fell against him.

"Like what?"

"Don't you know?"

The conversation was getting uncomfortable. Erin didn't like playing guessing games. Deliberately trying to change the subject, she righted herself and said, "Tell me more about yourself. Do you like to swim? To play tennis?"

"They're okay," Eddie said, then smiled at Erin. "I'd probably like them more if I did them with you."

Erin smiled back. "That could be arranged."

Eddie drove into a parking lot and turned his car over to a young attendant, who didn't try to disguise his expression of disgust. "Next time it will be a Bronco," Eddie

---

promised him. "You can park it right in front and impress the local community."

The attendant didn't respond and drove off so fast that the VW's tires squealed.

Eddie took Erin's hand and led her out of the lot, where their way was suddenly blocked by a half-dozen people who were heading toward their parked cars.

A heavy woman dressed in matching purple flowered pants and blouse screamed in Erin's face. "Look who it is!" she yelled at her companions. "Katie Norman!" Another piercing scream made Erin wince. "And Clarence! It's Clarence Nutweilder!"

The woman grabbed Erin's arm as the others pressed closer. "We came to L.A. to see celebrities, and we haven't seen anybody! And now—just the day before we have to fly back home—here you are! Is this lucky, or what!"

Erin tried unsuccessfully to tug her arm away. A blue-haired woman reached out and wound her fingers in Erin's hair. Erin tried to pull away, but the woman wouldn't let go.

"I touched her! I can tell everybody back home I touched her!" the woman shouted.

"We love watching your show, honey," a man said. He clapped a hand on Erin's shoulder for emphasis.

Erin jerked away in panic. As she staggered off balance, she lost her grip on Eddie's hand. She tried to make her way to his side, but she was surrounded. Their mouths were open, grinning, salivating, and their wide eyes glittered as they pushed closer. Terrified, Erin screamed, "Eddie! Help me!"

"Move back!" Eddie yelled, and she saw him trying to reach her. A woman was following him, digging in her heels as she clung to the collar of his shirt.

Eddie managed to thrust aside the man, who had clutched Erin's shoulder again, but Erin heard the sleeve of her blouse rip as part of it went with him.

"Lucky! You got a souvenir!" The woman attached to Eddie's shirt screeched and suddenly gave such a yank it pulled Eddie backward, gagging him.

The parking-lot attendant came at a run.

"Get the car!" Eddie yelled as he struggled to regain his balance.

The attendant wheeled, instantly obeying, shouting over his shoulder, "I called for help!"

It didn't take long for help to arrive. Two burly men, dressed as waiters, elbowed their way into the fracas and formed a barrier between Eddie and Erin and the tourists.

"I thought they'd be like they are on TV," the heavy woman shouted. "But they're snobs! Just snobs! What's with them that they can't be nice to a few fans?" She glared at Erin. "Who do you think you are? What makes you think you're so much better than other people? Wait till we get home and tell everybody what you're really like! Snobs! Celebrity snobs!"

The attendant raced up in Eddie's car, stopping so suddenly at the edge of the group that two people jumped back. One of the men hammered with his fist on the front fender and yelled an obscenity at Eddie.

"Get in the car," Eddie said to Erin. "Make it fast!"

As they drove out of the lot, the man managed to give

the car a loud parting blow. Erin ducked and protectively clapped her hands to her face, discovering that her cheeks were wet with tears.

She gave a loud sniff as she fumbled through her shoulder bag. She looked up, sniffing again, as she asked Eddie, "Have you got any tissues? My nose is going to run."

"It already has." She heard the laughter in his voice. "I've got a box of tissues in the glove compartment."

"It wasn't funny," she said, blowing her nose and mopping at her face as they drove down Beverly Boulevard.

"You're right. It wasn't funny. But your runny nose was." Eddie turned to examine her face. "You look a lot better now."

"Runny noses aren't funny either," she huffed. "They're embarrassing."

"I had to laugh at something," Eddie said seriously. "Or else start screaming. I was so scared that I was shaking."

"You were? Me, too. I didn't know when they'd stop. Maybe not until they'd pulled out my hair or torn off my arm." Erin held up her left hand, which was still trembling.

Eddie took it and held it tightly. "Remember when I said there were disadvantages to being an actor? What just happened was one of them. A big one."

"Why do people act like that?" Erin asked.

"I don't know, but some of them do." Eddie paused and asked, "Do you really want to go through your whole life like that? Not going to the places you'd like to go to? Hiding away from people who want to paw you and pull at you and grab for souvenirs?"

"But that doesn't happen very often."

"Often enough. Is the acting worth it? I honestly don't think it is for me."

Erin shook her head. Give up what meant the most in life? Turn away from acting because of monsters like those fans? Never! She couldn't! But she shuddered at the memory of the faces pushing into hers.

"Eddie," Erin whispered, too miserable to try to sort out her feelings, "could you park the car someplace? I'm still so shaky I know I'm going to start to cry again. It would help a lot if you could just hold me."

"Gladly," Eddie said. He made a right turn down the next street, which was lined with tall, slender palms and wide bursts of oleander, and parked under a streetlight in front of one of the white stucco houses.

"Hey, look, don't cry," Eddie said as he turned off the ignition. "You don't have to put up with people like that. You don't have to be an actress. Acting is such a closed-in business. There's a lot more to life, and you're missing out on it."

"No," Erin insisted. "I want to be an actress. I *have* to be an actress! And I'm not going to let horrible people stop me."

With Eddie's arms tightly around her and his lips against her forehead, Erin burst into angry tears.

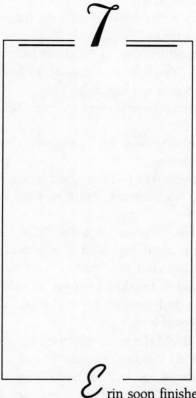

*7*

*E*rin soon finished crying. She sat up and blew her nose again.

"Are you okay now?" Eddie asked her.

Erin took a deep breath and nodded yes.

"I think you'll feel better if you get something to eat," Eddie said. "We're not dressed up enough for a place like Jimmy's or Perino's or any of the classy restaurants where we'd be safe from crazy fans. Want to order through a McDonald's drive-in window?"

"I have a better idea," Erin told him with a smile. "Let's go to my house."

Eddie leaned back to take a closer look at her, and his eyes twinkled. "You'll have to explain to Mrs. Hackett that the way you look is not my fault!"

"Mrs. Hackett won't even see me. She goes to bed early."

"She wouldn't come out to see who's there and hang around to chaperone?"

It hadn't occurred to Erin. She'd never brought a date home before. "No," she said, fairly sure she was right. "She wouldn't."

Eddie's eyes gleamed wickedly. "You mean there'd be nothing to stop me if I decided to kiss you?" He tucked a hand under Erin's chin and lifted it. "Like this?"

His lips barely brushed her own, so softly it was like a tickle that shivered through her body, and she found herself leaning toward him.

"Or like this?" His arms tightened around her, pulling her close, and his kiss was firm and tender.

Erin intended to remind Eddie that they were just friends, but it was impossible to speak, and it took only a few seconds for her to forget her resolve, to forget everything except the warmth of his mouth on hers.

She finally made herself pull away. Feeling as though she were coming up from the deep end of the swimming pool, she took a long, shuddering breath and opened her eyes.

"Eddie," she murmured, "we're going to be just friends. Remember?"

"I think that was a friendly kiss," he said.

"Well, I don't!"

He put on a mock expression of concern. "You think it was *unfriendly?*"

"No. I mean . . . Oh, you know what I mean."

His voice was low. "You kissed me back."

"I know."

"Would you do it again?"

His lips were so close. And Erin could smell the light, tangy fragrance of his shaving lotion. She lifted her chin as her answer.

"Maybe we'd better not," Eddie said. "Not here, anyway. I didn't know what it would be like to kiss you. I didn't know what it would do to me."

"I liked it, too," Erin admitted.

A nearby porch light flashed on. Eddie released Erin and reached to turn the ignition key. "Time to go," he said.

Erin leaned back against the lumpy seat, examining Eddie's profile from the corner of her eye. She hadn't thought of him as handsome, but she'd been wrong. Eddie *was* good-looking. Maybe she had let his role influence her. She reached up and tentatively touched her lips, which were still warm and tingly from Eddie's kiss. There was absolutely nothing about Eddie that was anything like Clarence.

She put the night's terrifying disturbance out of her mind. This was going to be a great evening.

When they arrived at Erin's house, the downstairs rooms were bright.

"Someone besides Mrs. Hackett must be here," Erin said as they climbed out of Eddie's car.

"If she's entertaining anyone, she won't want extra guests," Eddie said. "I'd better just say good night now."

With satisfaction, Erin heard the reluctance in his voice. She took his hand and pulled him toward the front door. "Mrs. Hackett doesn't give parties. Maybe Abby's here. C'mon. We'll find out who it is."

She heard her mother's voice the minute she and Eddie had crossed the entry hall.

"Mom?" she called out eagerly, and ran into the living room.

"Erin!" As Cassie whirled to greet Erin, the smile froze on her face, and her eyes widened. She looked from Erin to Eddie and back to Erin. "Erin," she managed to stammer, "your—your clothes are torn!"

Marc strode into the room and stopped short, the same look of amazement and concern in his eyes.

"I know that, and I'm going to tell you why," Erin said, trying to keep the irritation from her voice. This wasn't exactly the loving homecoming it should have been. "Before we get to that, I want to introduce you to Eddie Jarvis."

"I'm pleased to meet you," Eddie said, but there was only a stunned silence.

"It's all right if you say hello to me," Eddie told them. He spoke in a voice that wobbled between his own and Clarence Nutweilder's, adding, "The way Erin looks is not my fault."

Everyone began talking at once. Erin was glad that her parents were embarrassed. Why couldn't they have just said "Hi" to Eddie and hugged her and told her they missed her? Why did her mom have to make such a big thing about the way she looked?

But Erin gasped as she caught sight of her reflection in the gilt-framed mirror that hung over a Queen Anne side table. Her hair was a tangled mess, her cheeks were streaked with mascara, and the area around her mouth was smudged with lipstick. She had to admit that her mother had a right to wonder.

Cassie wrapped her arms around Erin, and Erin hugged her back. "You're home a week early," she said. "Why didn't you let me know you'd be coming?"

"We did," Cassie said. "I wrote and told you there was a strong possibility we'd be home early. It was in the letter you left unopened on the hall table."

"Oh," Erin said. "That letter. Well, I didn't get it until late today. I was going to open it later."

"It doesn't matter," Marc said, and kissed her, his beard tickling her cheek. "We're here, and we're glad to be home, and we've missed you, sweetheart."

"I missed you, too. I always do," Erin said, suddenly realizing how glad she was to see her parents again. She clung to both of them. "I can't wait to hear all about the filming."

"I'd better be going," Eddie interrupted.

Cassie reached into the pocket of her skirt and pulled out a tissue, handing it to Eddie. A smile flickered at the corners of her mouth. "You might want to wipe the lipstick off your face," she said.

Eddie groaned and did as she suggested. "I think I'll stay," he said, "at least until Erin explains what happened."

"That might be a good idea," Cassie answered.

Erin plopped onto one of the sofas, and Eddie sat beside her. As she recounted the story, recalling her fear, she reached for his hand and held it tightly.

When she finished, her father shook his head sadly, and her mother said, "This isn't the kind of childhood I wanted for you."

"I'm not a child," Erin protested.

Cassie didn't respond to that. "Honey," she said, "as long as your face is before the public you won't have any privacy, and you know that. Horrible situations like the one you just went through will occur over and over again. It isn't worth it, is it?"

"Of course it is!"

"Ouch," Eddie muttered as he tugged his fingers away.

"Be honest with yourself, Erin. You told us how frightened you were," Cassie said.

"I know, but . . ."

"Do you really want to live like that?"

"Yes, I do!" Erin jumped to her feet. "Mom, you don't understand how much I . . ."

Marc stood, too. "This is not the time to discuss it. Erin and Eddie haven't had anything to eat, and I wouldn't mind having a sandwich myself. Why don't we go into the kitchen and see what's on hand?"

"No, thanks," Eddie answered as he got to his feet. "I'd better be getting home."

Cassie smiled warmly at him. "I admit we didn't give you much of a welcome, but we're glad you're here, Eddie. We really are," she said. "Please don't hurry off."

"Thanks, but I really ought to go—" Eddie said, looking from Erin to her parents.

"We're glad to have met you, Eddie," Marc interrupted.

Erin waited impatiently for her parents to say all the usual polite things before she walked outside with Eddie. She firmly closed the door, put her arms around Eddie's neck, and looked into his eyes. "I'm sorry," she said.

"Don't be sorry," he answered. "Your parents are nice people. They were just worried about you, that's all." He grinned. "You'll understand why they reacted the way they did when you look in a mirror."

"I saw," she told him. "There's a mirror over one of the tables." She smiled, and murmured, "What I was going to say was I'm sorry my parents interrupted our evening. I was hoping you'd kiss me again."

"In the dark it was pretty nice, but once I got a good look at you in the light, no chance," he said as his arms tightened around her.

"No chance?" she repeated, her lips nearly touching his.

"Well, maybe a small one," he murmured, and his kiss was as wonderful as Erin had remembered, so overwhelming that she didn't want it to end.

This time it was Eddie who pulled away. "Can I pick

you up tomorrow? Will you come to John's party with me?" he whispered against her ear.

"Oh, yes," she answered. The beach, the moonlight on the ocean . . . a perfect place to be with Eddie.

After Eddie had driven away, Erin remained in the small, shadowy porch outside the front door. She needed time to be alone, to try to figure out what had happened to her. From the moment Eddie had been cast in a regular role as Katie Norman's boyfriend, she and Eddie had been friends.

Only tonight she wasn't thinking of Eddie as just a friend. Was this love? No, although thinking of his kisses made her breathe faster. Could she fall in love with Eddie? Maybe. Maybe not. Unable to understand her mixed-up feelings, Erin opened the door and walked back into the house.

Erin stopped to glance into the living-room mirror as she ran to answer the doorbell the next evening. Her hair was shining, and the pink and white cotton knit sweater, top, and skirt she was wearing reflected the pink in her cheeks. She looked good. She felt good. She was looking forward both to seeing Eddie and to attending the wrap party. It was going to be a wonderful evening.

"What an improvement!" Eddie teased as Erin opened the door. He greeted her parents, promised to bring Erin back safely at a reasonable hour, waited while she kissed her parents good night, and led her to his car.

She slid over on the seat so that she was close to him. "I'm avoiding that broken spring," she explained.

"That's why I haven't fixed it," he answered.

The drive from Bel-Air to Malibu didn't take long, and on the way they chatted about the show.

"I've grown up on it," Erin said. "I can't imagine another way of life." She paused, then added, "And I always feel a little sad at the wrap party. I know I won't be working with my TV family for nearly four months."

"What are you going to do in the meantime?" Eddie asked.

"Whatever my agent comes up with. He thinks I've got a good chance for a commercial that's in the works." She sighed, and added, "I wish I had a movie lined up, like Marcie does."

"Not me," Eddie said. "Next week I'll buy my Bronco, and then I'm off to the Big Sur, northern California redwood country. It's beautiful, Erin. When I close my eyes, I can imagine myself already there, with quiet all around me, and I can even smell the salty mist that rolls in from the sea."

Erin felt a sharp pang of loneliness and wished he weren't going. "How long will you be away?" she asked.

He reached over and took her hand. "Not long," he said. "Just long enough to get my life straightened out."

"What does that mean?"

"Erin, this past year on *The Family Next Door* was my big break in television, but now that it's over I've reached a turning point. I'd like to get away from this town so that I can remember what's really important."

"To me, this town is important," Erin told him.

"There's a lot more to life than the next day's script

changes or the next season's show. The farther away you get from them, the less important they seem."

Erin shook her head. "I don't agree."

"Acting's the biggest thing in your life?"

"Of course."

He turned to her with a mournful expression. "I was hoping you'd say it was me."

"There are lots of things that are important," Erin teased. "You're near the top of the list." She stretched to aim a kiss near his cheek.

"Just keep that in mind," Eddie said with a grin. He let go of Erin's hand in order to make the turn onto the coast highway.

A few minutes later, they stopped at the gates of the Colony and were waved through. They parked near John Haywood's brightly lit beachfront house and were ushered into the party by a beautiful, dark-haired woman he introduced as his wife, Lily.

"What happened to the wife he brought to the set last October?" Eddie whispered to Erin.

"She wasn't his wife. They were going to get married, but they broke up."

"So this one is the third?"

"Fourth."

Eddie shrugged. "See what I mean? This town does strange things to people."

"Don't blame Hollywood." Erin brushed a strand of hair from her eyes, turning so that the ocean breeze blew it away from her face. She could hear the hissing of wavelets from the dark water as they slid up the sand just a few feet from the deck where they stood, and she could smell the sharp, clean salt spray. "Listen," she said. "You can hear the ocean right here in Malibu, and you can smell it, too."

"It's not the same as in Big Sur."

"It's the same ocean."

He leaned over the railing and pretended to gape. "It can't be!"

Erin laughed. "Be serious."

Eddie pulled off his shoes and tossed them into a corner.

"What are you doing?" Erin asked.

"Come on," he said. "Let's run along the sand. Let's get our feet wet. Take your shoes off, too."

Tina arrived, and her mother allowed her to join their play. They tagged and yelled and raced up to the waves and back again.

"The children are occupied," Marcie said loudly to Jake, so that Erin could overhear her.

"Why don't we go down there and do what they're doing?" Jake asked.

"You've got to be kidding!" Marcie turned away with a sniff, not letting go of Jake's hand and tugging him back inside the house.

Erin didn't mind Marcie's remark. She was having too much fun to care what Marcie said or did.

Eventually the steaks were cooked and eaten, and finally people began thanking John and Lily and leaving the party.

"Stick around," John quietly told Erin and Eddie. "I'd like to say a few words to the cast." That explained why

John hadn't made his usual, sweetly corny speech earlier in the evening. This year, he was sparing the crew.

Erin sat with Eddie on one of the sofas in the living room, and Tina snuggled between them. As Tina prattled on, retelling in great detail the entire plot of the Roger Rabbit cartoon she'd just seen, Erin studied the others. Marcie seemed totally unconcerned with anything or anyone except Jake, but his eyes met Erin's, and he winked.

*What an ego!* she thought as she looked away. Tina's mother was chatting with Lydia and Lily, Gene with John, but the lighthearted mood of the party had vanished.

At last John invited the others to be seated and perched on the edge of a large lounge chair, facing them.

"At a wrap party, we always thank everyone involved in the show during the past year's work. And tonight I want to give all of you an extra thank-you, because you're the ones who were responsible for making the show a continued success."

For just a moment, John looked down at his hands, and Erin imagined she saw him frown; but when he looked up, his expression was serene. "Many shows falter right from the start. Many of them begin with great publicity and hoopla, then fade in a hurry. We can all be proud of the fact that *The Family Next Door* began in the top ten and is going out, four years later, still in the top ten."

It took a moment for what he said to register. "Going out?" Erin cried. "What are you telling us?"

"I can't believe that the network would cancel us!" Tina's mother's shrill voice took on a pleading tone. "Maybe if we all went to talk to—to whomever made the decision, we could change his mind."

Gene stood up, interrupting. "Lydia and I made the decision," he said.

Erin gasped.

"That's right," Lydia said. She stood beside Gene, her hands held out as though in petition, and Erin could see them tremble. "I know it's a hard choice, but maybe I can explain." She took a deep breath, looked as though she were praying for the right words, and said, "The structure of the show changed. You know that."

Marcie stiffened. "If you're blaming me because I became the star of the show—"

But Gene didn't give her a chance to continue. "Remember how it was in the beginning? The idea was pitched to us as a family show, with strong parts for the parents, and there was going to be a lot of humor with Lydia's—Nancy Norman's—pregnancy. The kids were cute and funny and got in our hair, and the audience was supposed to identify with the parents."

"But it changed," Lydia repeated with a conciliatory smile and nod toward Marcie. "When Marcie became such a hot property in films, the shows began to revolve around her. Our audience changed, too. It became younger. The fans write for pictures of the kids." Her smile shifted to Jake. "And this season Jake has become some kind of a sex symbol with the junior-high-school crowd."

"Well, hey," Jake said, and bowed to the right and the left as though he were winning an award.

---

"I don't understand," Tina's mother said. "If the show's still popular, does it matter?"

"It does to us," Gene told her. "Mrs. Reed, Lydia is a tremendously talented actress, and I can truthfully say that I'm not so bad myself. How do you think we like having our parts limited to walking in and out of the kitchen while our kids are carrying the action?"

Lydia broke in. "And saying clever things like 'Good night, kids' or 'Do you really think Andrea's getting serious with Bill?' "

She shook her head sadly, and Erin could see the tears in Lydia's eyes. "Gene and I have been offered roles to die for," she said, "and our contracts were up for renewal for *The Family Next Door,* so we decided not to renew."

John broke in. "They talked it over with me," he said. "I didn't like to see the show end, but I had to agree with them." He looked at Gene. "Gene's been offered the lead in an espionage series on another network. It's a great part."

"And Lydia's going to Broadway," Gene said.

"Theater is my first love," Lydia murmured. "I think you all know that. And *The Family Next Door* doesn't even use a studio audience for the Friday tapings, as many situation comedies do."

Erin spoke up. "John, you said the story in *Snoop* was only a rumor."

John ran a hand through his hair and looked embarrassed. "I didn't admit to anything," he said. "I couldn't. How that gossip sheet got the information before we were ready to break it, I don't know, but I couldn't let it affect the cast. You would all have been so down while we filmed the last shows, your mood would have come across to the viewers."

Gene sat down again, and Lydia followed. "I know it's tough, but you're all talented actors," Gene said. "There's no doubt about Marcie's career. She's headed right for the top. And Jake, did you tell them you were cutting a record?"

As Jake grinned, Gene turned to Erin, Eddie, and Tina. "Nothing's going to stop the three of you," he said. "One of these days, you'll probably outshine us all."

Eddie was saying something encouraging. What it was Erin didn't know. All she heard was the tone of his voice. Erin knew she should smile and reassure Gene. She should try to erase the guilt in Lydia's eyes. She concentrated on what she should tell them. *Congratulations, both of you. It's wonderful. We're proud of you.* Yes. That would sound right.

But just as she opened her mouth, Tina looked up at her with sorrowful eyes and wailed, "Erin, does that mean you won't be my sister anymore?"

Erin buried her face against Tina's hair, unable to say a single word.

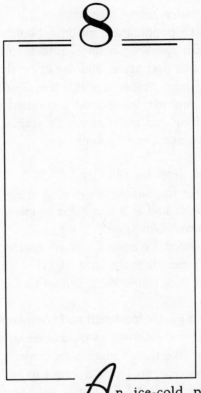

*8*

*A*n ice-cold pain crawled through Erin's arms and legs and settled into a frozen lump that pressed against her lungs. It hurt to breathe, it hurt to think, but Erin didn't have time to give in to the pain. She felt herself being jerked to her feet and heard Eddie say, "That's great news for you, Lydia. And for you, Gene. Hey! Why are we just sitting here? Shouldn't we break out the champagne?"

"Champagne! Of course! Coming right up," John responded, his voice hearty with relief.

It was like popping a cork on a bottle of hubbub, as everyone began speaking at once. Erin found herself being hugged over and over again, and she knew she was hugging in return and managing to mumble the right things. By the time glasses were handed around and raised in a toast, she was able to think and see clearly once again.

"To Lydia and Gene," John said.

"To success."

"To good times for all of us."

Erin spoke up, her voice catching as she said, "To the good times we've had as a family for so many years."

"Hear, hear," Gene said.

Lydia beamed. "We were a pretty special family."

"Hey, it's not all in the past, right?" Erin said quickly. "We'll still see each other. We'll still go on being a family in spirit."

Mrs. Reed gave a loud sigh and complained to John, "I just can't believe the network would agree to end a successful show, just like that. Couldn't we make some changes? Maybe have the parents go on a long trip and the kids stay with an aunt and uncle? Or just recast the parents' parts? They did that on Valerie Harper's show when she asked for too much money."

John gestured toward Marcie. "It wouldn't work. Marcie's agent has been letting us know that she can make more in films than with the show. We'd be down to just the two younger girls."

Lydia stepped forward. "This has been a wonderful

party, but I must leave," she said. "After indulging in all that wonderful food, I'm practically asleep on my feet."

"It's time for me to leave, too," Gene said, and the two of them began another round of hugs.

As she held Gene tightly, Erin said, "We'll all get together soon. Right?"

"Absolutely," he said, and turned to shake Jake's hand.

"When?" Erin asked, but no one seemed to hear her.

"Come on," Eddie said in her ear. "It's time to go."

Tina tugged at Erin's arm and raised her hands for one more hug. As Erin bent to kiss her, Tina said, "You'll still take me to the zoo, won't you?"

"Absolutely," Erin said quickly. She gasped as she realized that without thinking she'd repeated Gene's own answer. She looked into Tina's troubled eyes and said, "We'll do something fun together. I promise."

As Erin walked with Eddie to his car, she said, "I wonder if this is what it feels like when your parents get divorced."

"No, it isn't," Eddie answered firmly.

"I guess you're right," she said, surprised at the bitterness she heard in her voice. "At least in a divorce, you can stay with one parent. Neither of these parents wants to keep us."

Eddie looked into Erin's eyes as he opened the car door for her. "What's with you?" he asked. "Don't talk like Lydia and Gene are your real parents, because they're not."

"But they're close to it," she said. She settled herself near the driver's seat, away from the broken spring, and waited until Eddie was seated next to her before she added,

"I've grown up with them. During most of each year, I've worked with them every day. I'm with them twice as much as I'm with my own parents."

Eddie took her chin in one hand and with the other made a pass in the air as though he were a hypnotist. In a deep voice, he said, "Then tell yourself, 'It's only a movie. It's only a movie.' "

"I would, if I could just believe it," Erin said.

Marcie and Jake left the house, crossed the drive in front of them, and climbed into a low, black Jaguar.

"Then tell yourself, 'I'm getting rid of Marcie,' " Eddie said. "That ought to help." After two attempts, he managed to start his car and pulled out into the street.

Erin said wistfully, "Marcie and I used to have fun together when the show started. She only began acting like a snob this last year."

"Then be glad you won't have to put up with it any longer."

Erin found herself defending Marcie. "Sisters don't always get along with each other."

For a few minutes, Eddie concentrated on the highway traffic before he said, "Look, Erin, you can make yourself miserable by trying to convince yourself that this bunch of actors was like a real family, or you can tell yourself it was just a job, and there will be other jobs, other 'parents,' other 'families.' "

"I'm not trying to make myself miserable." Erin moved away from Eddie, preferring the broken spring that poked into her thigh to being so close to him. "You don't understand," she said. "You've only been on the show this last year, and that's because the writers thought I needed a boyfriend, too. But Lydia and Gene have been like real parents to me since I was twelve."

"They've been good friends," he said. "You've already got a set of parents—a complete set."

"Like salt and pepper shakers. They go together with no room for anyone in between."

The car screeched to a stoplight, and Eddie turned to Erin, his forehead and cheekbones highlighted in the red glow, his eyes dim in the night shadows. "Why should you be *between* them?"

Flustered, Erin stammered, "I—I didn't mean it that way. I—I meant . . ."

"I met your parents. Remember? They're nice people, and it was easy to see that they care very much about you."

"Don't lecture me, Eddie." Erin knew her face was pink with embarrassment. In her irritation, she could feel it grow even warmer. "You don't know anything about it."

There was a long pause while Eddie turned the car onto Sunset Boulevard. Finally, he said, "I know what it's like to be unwanted. I already told you about my mother. I haven't seen my father since I was three years old."

"I'm sorry," Erin said. She wished she were home. She didn't want to hear Eddie scold her. She didn't want to hear about his problems. She felt like she did when she'd been six and had fallen on her roller skates. For a while her arm had been so numb that she hadn't felt the pain, but when the numbness had worn off, her arm had hurt so much that she'd screamed and screamed. Only then had her nanny realized it was broken.

That's how it was now. The numbness was rapidly sliding away, and the hurt was raw. *The Family Next Door* was over. It wouldn't begin again next year. It was really over. The major part of her life had actually ended, and there was nothing she could do to change it.

She didn't speak. She couldn't. And Eddie seemed unwilling to continue the conversation. It wasn't until he pulled up in front of her house and walked her to the front door that he said, "Erin, if you need me, just call me. Okay?"

He reached out to hold her, but Erin stiffened. If she let down for even a second, she knew she'd burst into tears.

Eddie stepped back. "That's the way it is?"

When Erin didn't respond, he turned and loped down the walk to his car.

"Eddie!" Erin tried to call out, but the word was lost in a rush of tears.

As Eddie's car pulled away from the curb, Erin turned and fumbled with the door key, sobbing and crying as she blindly tried to find the lock. She managed to turn the key and fling herself into the house, locking the door behind her.

"Erin?" She heard her mother's heels on the tile in the entry hall and ran to her, glad for the security of her mother's arms around her.

"Are you hurt?" Cassie asked, her voice shrill with fear.

Erin shook her head.

"Where's Eddie?"

"It's not Eddie's fault," Erin said. "Just hold me, Mom."

Cassie did, her arms tightening, and in a few minutes

the urgency of Erin's sobs began to slide away as though a knot had been untied. After a few, final, shuddering hiccups, Erin was able to raise her head. She wiped the back of her hand across her eyes and gave a loud snuffle.

"Here," Cassie said as she pulled a tissue from the pocket of her blouse. "Use this."

Erin swiped at her eyes and blew her nose loudly.

"Honey, can you tell me now what this is all about?" Cassie asked.

Erin nodded. "You don't have to look so scared, Mom."

"I *am* scared," Cassie told her. "I've never seen you in such a state."

She took Erin's hand and led her to a nearby sofa, skirting an array of color prints and slides that she'd arranged in a pattern on the floor.

"You're working, and I interrupted you," Erin said.

"It doesn't matter. It's not that important. *You're* important," Cassie assured her. "Can I get you something? How about a cup of hot cocoa?"

Erin made a face. "No, thanks. I'm not a little kid." She took her mother's hands in her own, not wanting to let go, as though she were drowning and had to cling tightly to something. She gulped a deep breath and said, "We got the word tonight. *The Family Next Door* has been canceled."

"It's been canceled?" Erin could see that her mother was so surprised that it was hard for her to realize what Erin had said.

"Lydia and Gene aren't going to sign new contracts. Lydia's going back to New York, and Gene was offered the lead in some kind of a spy series."

Cassie let out a long breath of air and leaned back against the sofa. "Well, well," she said. "It couldn't have happened at a better time."

"What are you talking about?"

Cassie smiled. "College, sweetheart. You can have a real senior year in high school and then go on to college. Your grades have been excellent, so you could apply to USC, our alma mater. Marc and I would love that."

Erin jumped off the sofa and stood in front of her mother. "Mom! I tell you the show's ended, and you act glad and start talking about USC! It's like somebody tells you her husband died, and you say, 'It couldn't come at a better time. Now you can marry somebody else.' "

Cassie got to her feet, too. "That's not the same thing at all."

"Isn't it? For four years, I worked on that show. I was in every episode, and Lydia and Gene and Marcie and Tina were my family. I remember how excited I was when Lydia had a baby. It was like having a real little sister. It was the only way I was going to know what having a little sister was like."

Cassie flushed, but her eyes didn't leave Erin's. "The people you worked with were fine people," she said. "If they weren't, I wouldn't have allowed you to be on the show. But the family was imaginary. Marc and I, we're your parents, not Lydia and Gene."

For an instant Erin looked away, suddenly aware of how much she'd hurt her mother. "I'm sorry," she said. "I didn't mean it the way it sounded."

"Oh, Erin," Cassie said, dropping back to the sofa as

though her legs had given way, "I think I understand how unhappy you feel about the program being over. Whether you want to admit it or not, it was inevitable, if not this year, then maybe next year or the next. That's one of the problems your father and I wanted to spare you. An actor's life is hard enough, but it's such a confusing, artificial world for a child actor."

"I'm not a child."

"You were when you began the show. Face facts, Erin. At seventeen, you're not exactly an adult." She held out a hand. "Sit down, sweetheart. Let's talk some more."

Erin shook her head and took a step backward. "I don't want to talk right now."

"Maybe if we talk, it will help you. This problem is not as bad as it seems. As I told you, it might be a blessing in disguise."

Erin felt her face grow warm with anger. "I don't want to hear about how I can have a *real* senior year in high school and go to USC."

"If you wouldn't resist everything I tell you, if you'd just give me a chance to explain—"

Erin exploded. "What you want is for me to live the kind of life you lived, to be a carbon copy of you! To go to the proper private school and zero in on a career that has nothing to do with Hollywood! You want me to be your kind of success, but I want my own kind of life! I want to be an actress!"

"Don't shout, Erin. We can't talk if you're going to shout."

"We can't talk at all," Erin said. "You don't understand the first thing about me."

"I'm afraid, the way you're carrying on, that no one could."

Erin suddenly stopped, stared at her mother, and in a quiet voice said, "Yes, there is someone who could. Abby could."

For a few moments, Cassie was silent. "Oh?" Cassie said. "Do you think so?" Erin was shocked by the emptiness in her mother's voice. "I'm Abby's daughter, and she was never able to understand me."

## 9

*I*t was late the next afternoon before Erin could visit Abby. She found her grandmother out by the pool, lying on a lounge, totally covered by a large orange-and-yellow-striped beach towel.

"Who's there?" Abby asked, her voice muffled by the towel.

"It's me, Erin." She perched on a webbed chair next to Abby.

Abby lifted the towel and peered out at Erin. "Want a swim?"

"Later," Erin said. She paused. "You know, it doesn't do any good to lie out in the sun if you're all covered up."

"It's a nice, warm way to take a nap," Abby said. She threw back the towel and sat up. "Too much sun can ruin your skin. It's never too early to learn that little fact of life."

Erin nodded, and Abby said, "Have you had anything to eat? There's some pasta salad in the refrigerator."

"No, thanks," Erin said. "Abby, I need to talk to you."

As Abby stood, Erin noticed that her grandmother's body was still in good shape, a little thicker around the middle, but her legs were firm and slender. Abby refused to admit she'd had face-lifts and neck surgery to tighten her sagging chin, preferring to keep up the pretense she'd been "out of town" at those times. But whatever her grandmother had done, Erin thought, she looked great.

"If we're going to talk, then let's go inside the house," Abby said. She slipped her arms into a voluminous terry-cloth robe and led the way through the patio to the sun room.

Once they had been comfortably seated and Dolores had brought frosted glasses of iced tea, decorated with mint leaves from Abby's garden, Erin blurted out, "*The Family Next Door* is over."

"I know," Abby said, although there was a question in her voice as she studied Erin.

"Not for the season," Erin wailed. "Forever." She went on to tell Abby about Lydia's and Gene's plans.

"I'm sorry, Erin," Abby said. "I know how much it

hurts. It always hurts when a show ends, especially when you aren't expecting it." She took a long swallow of tea and settled her glass into a coaster on the end table.

"I knew you'd understand," Erin told her.

But Abby didn't seem to hear. "I can still remember when they told me that the networks had canceled my first situation comedy. I had seen it coming, with the ratings steadily falling, but I hadn't wanted to admit it to myself."

"Abby, it's different. Our ratings were still high."

"But there it was. Just like getting socked in the stomach. I felt physically sick."

"So did I. I thought I'd pass out. I—"

"I came home and went to bed and stayed there all day. Bobby tried to get me to come down to dinner, and I was horrible to poor Bobby, who was trying to make me feel better. But I just couldn't help it."

Erin didn't want to think of how she had acted with Eddie and with Cassie. "Nobody really understands, Abby."

Abby patted Erin's hand. "Nobody understands except those who've gone through it."

Erin struggled to put her feelings into words. "It's like—like having your family move away and leave you behind. It's—it's just like being deserted." She gave a long sigh, relieved at having finally given expression to the misery that had been tormenting her, and picked up her iced-tea glass, scarcely aware of the damp chill under her fingertips.

"Deserted?" Abby repeated. One eyebrow arched, and she smiled. "That gives me a good idea. We can find a deserted island and put all the little pinhead network creeps on it and leave them there forever without their telephone pages at the Polo Lounge and their big glass offices filled with charts and graphs and Nielsen ratings and yes-men." She paused. "Who else do you want on that island? Lydia and Gene?"

"No!" Erin answered. She stared down at her hands. "They were like my own—like another set of parents. I can't blame them for what they want to do. I just . . . well, I'm going to miss them." Almost shyly, she said to Abby, "I really care about them, and I know they care about me."

Abby nodded. "You made a lot of good friends on the set, and you'll make more on your next show."

"Mom doesn't want there to be a 'next show.' Her exact words were that this cancellation was a blessing. As Mom put it, now I can have a *real* senior year in high school and go on to college."

"Your mother probably has the right idea," Abby said.

"No!" Erin shouted.

"Why not? You're hurting right now, and you're wondering where and when your next acting job will be. That's not good for someone your age." Abby shook her head slowly. "There's a lot of worry and pain in the acting business. An actor is out of work more than he's in work. It's a tough, miserable life. I should never have encouraged you to go into it."

"But you always loved it."

Abby shrugged. "I never claimed to have good sense."

"You know you love acting," Erin said. "You told me how you worked to develop your own career, and I've tried so hard to be like you."

Abby struggled to climb out of the deep lounger. "I didn't do you any favors, did I, when I helped you walk into a career without having to work hard to get it?"

Erin gasped, stunned at what Abby had said. "I was *good* at the audition! That's why they picked me!"

"Of course you were good," Abby said. "I knew you would be, or I wouldn't have sent you." She cocked her head and studied Erin. "But surely you realized you had an extra edge on the other girls, didn't you?"

Erin, still in shock, could only stammer, "I—I guess."

"It takes more than talent to make things happen in this town," Abby said. "Believe me, I know." Abby shrugged. "Have you got what it takes to make it all happen for yourself? Probably, but maybe it's better that you don't know and don't try. You can see what happened to me, Erin. Inside I feel young, but I'm told that I'm old. I feel the same zing, the same talent, and I want to make people laugh, but I'm told that what I do is out of date and no one is interested. 'You've made lots of money,' they say, 'so relax and enjoy it.'" Her voice caught as she added, "But what I enjoy is being in front of the cameras, playing to an audience, giving my all and getting that wonderful response in return."

Erin found it hard to speak. "Abby, I can't believe you'd give up so easily."

"You think it was easy?" Abby's eyes flashed. "Believe me, it was anything but easy."

Erin jumped up and hugged her grandmother. "I'm sorry. I didn't mean it like that. I'm just trying to take in what you've just said. I thought you'd encourage me. I thought—"

"Oh, honey, you came for encouragement, and I didn't give you any," Abby said mournfully. "I let you down because I haven't anything left to give you." She released her hold on Erin and held her at arm's length, her big eyes on Erin's. "But maybe it's better this way. Listen to your mother. Give her way a chance."

"I want to be an actress," Erin said stubbornly, but Abby didn't answer.

Abby walked with Erin to the front door, pausing only by the hall table to pick up a book. "Oh, here," Abby said. "You told me you borrowed this from Lydia. It was fabulous. I read it in one sitting, and it actually took my mind off my troubles. You'll probably want to return it before Lydia leaves L.A."

Erin tucked the novel into her left elbow, gave Abby a routine good-bye kiss, and climbed into her car. Mercifully, it was a short drive home, because Erin couldn't keep her mind on the road and traffic. She was so disappointed and discouraged that all she wanted to do was what Abby had once done—climb into bed, hugging her misery around her, and stay away from all those people in her life who couldn't possibly understand it.

She couldn't get Abby's question out of her mind. "Have you got what it takes to make it all happen for yourself?" Erin hadn't answered the question. She didn't know the answer, and the way things were going, she wondered if she'd ever be able to find out.

\* \* \*

Erin took and passed her exams in English, math, biology, and American history. By fulfilling the required number of class days and hours set by the state of California, she had avoided making an appearance at a regular school every year. Now she'd have to go back to school if she weren't working on a show or a film.

Hoping that Zack would call with a job—at least with an audition—Erin flopped on her bed one morning within arm's reach of the phone. Lydia's copy of *The Dorchesters* lay on her nightstand, where it had been since Abby returned it. Erin picked it up and absently began reading.

It was a terrific story, just as Lydia and Abby had said. Soon Erin was totally absorbed. A couple of times she laughed out loud, and more than once the conflict between Judith, the grandmother, and Kim, her granddaughter, who felt unloved and unwanted, moved her so deeply that she burst into tears. Judith was a wealthy recluse living in a cocoon she'd built to protect herself from the unhappiness of the world. Kim, the granddaughter she didn't even know about, had shown up on her doorstep one day. Kim's father had insisted before his death that Kim should live with his estranged mother.

Erin identified with Kim, who mourned her dead parents and wanted her own independence, and who regretted the promise she'd made to a father who seemed to want to control her life even after his death.

Erin cried with joy when Judith and Kim finally broke down the barriers they'd built and were reconciled, but she sobbed brokenheartedly when Kim discovered the secret Judith had tried to keep from her.

---

She finished the last page, put down the book, and wiped her eyes. What a great story! Hadn't someone said *The Dorchesters* had been optioned by Orion? Or had they said it might be? It was a real tearjerker of a story and would make a terrific movie. The role of the teenaged granddaughter was a marvelous one. Marcie probably would get it, just as she got everything else she wanted.

Without the book to distract her any longer, Erin realized how much she missed Eddie, who hadn't telephoned. "If you need me, just call me," he'd told her. She clenched her teeth as she recalled the moment. *Not on your life,* she thought. *I'd call and get another lecture. Or, probably, no one would answer. By this time you'll be up in your precious Big Sur country, with everything else shut out of your life— including me.*

Erin jumped each time the telephone rang. Could it be Gene? Lydia? Maybe even Eddie? Surely Lydia—her other mother for four years—would call her to say good-bye. Wouldn't she?

Finally, Erin couldn't wait any longer, and on Thursday evening she decided to telephone Lydia. First she rehearsed what she would say. *I finished* The Dorchesters. *I know you'll want it back before you leave. Maybe we could get together for lunch.* Yes. That sounded right. Erin finally dialed the number, only to get a clipped, nasal recorded voice from the telephone company saying, "This number is no longer in service."

Her fingers trembling, Erin telephoned Gene. After a few moments of conversation, she said, "Lydia's already left Los Angeles."

"Sure," he said. "I think she was planning to go right away."

"I didn't know. You see, I have this book she lent me, *The Dorchesters,* and she'll probably want it back." Erin cringed, knowing that what she had said probably had sounded stupid.

"Oh, yeah," Gene said. "I remember. Some big, tearful novel, wasn't it? I heard that Elizabeth Taylor wanted to option it, but it fell through. Her studio thought the story was too much of a woman's story and wouldn't draw the crowds." He interrupted himself. "Naw. It couldn't have been Liz. Maybe Jane Fonda. Now, who was it told me that?"

Erin smiled at Gene's familiar rambling, but she didn't want to talk about the novel. "I thought maybe we could get together," she said.

"You mean the gang? That might be hard to do. Looks like we're all scattered." His voice picked up interest. "Hey, did you hear they increased the budget on that flick Marcie's in? Looks like she's going to get real star billing."

He went on to add more studio gossip before Erin could politely end the conversation. Gene didn't want to see her any more than Lydia had.

As she hung up the phone, she put her head in her hands. She *had* been deserted. It wasn't just a feeling. It was a reality. Her job, her security, her *family*—they'd all been taken away from her.

She began to close her address book, but one of the names caught her eye: Tina Reed. Was Tina also waiting and hoping that someone from her television family would call?

Erin closed the book. The last thing she wanted to do was to make an effort to be cheerful as she talked to Tina. But she thought of the little girl's face, the despair in her eyes as she had asked, "Does this mean you won't be my sister anymore?"

Erin opened her address book to the page with Tina's telephone number on it and picked up the phone.

Tina's mother answered, and she was surprisingly cordial to Erin. "She's missed you," Mrs. Reed said. Her voice changed to a contented purr as she added, "Of course, she's been kept so busy making commercials that it's helped to keep her mind off the cancellation of *The Family Next Door.*"

"That's good," Erin said. "Is Tina there? Could I speak to her?"

Mrs. Reed went on as though she hadn't heard Erin. "Tina's agent thinks he can land a part for her in a new series CBS is planning as a midseason replacement. I certainly hope so. If Lydia and Gene had just given us more notice, we might have been able to get Tina tested for a kid part in one of the fall shows."

"Mrs. Reed, I'm sure they didn't mean to—"

"How about you, Erin?" Tina's mother interrupted. "Have you got anything lined up?"

"Not much," Erin said reluctantly, "but my agent is working on it."

Mrs. Reed sighed and said, "Well, don't get discouraged, dear. I'm sure something will turn up."

The longer she talked to Mrs. Reed, the more depressed Erin grew. She quickly said, "I'd like to talk to Tina, please. But first, is it all right with you if I ask her to go to the zoo with me tomorrow?"

There was a short gasp before Mrs. Reed said, "Oh, dear me, that's impossible. You'd be mobbed in a public place."

"I realize that," Erin said, "but it's a school day, so first thing in the morning the zoo won't be crowded, and with some wigs and stage makeup and the right wardrobe, I could disguise us enough so that no one would recognize us. Tina told me how much she wants to go to the zoo."

There was a long pause while Erin assumed Mrs. Reed was thinking about it. Finally, Mrs. Reed said, "Are you that good with stage makeup?"

"I think so," Erin answered. With a flash of inspiration, she said, "I'll ask Abby to help."

She'd been right. The magic name had convinced Mrs. Reed. "Well, perhaps, in that case," she said slowly, "but you understand that I'll have to go with you."

Erin winced. The last thing in the world she wanted to do was spend a morning with Mrs. Reed. "I can take good care of Tina," she said.

"You don't realize," Mrs. Reed explained. "I never let Tina out of my sight."

"She won't feel that she and I are having an adventure if you're with us."

"Then I'll stay in the background," Mrs. Reed said. "But I do have to be on hand."

"Okay," Erin agreed. "I can be over at your house early to apply the disguise. About eight-thirty?"

"That will be fine," Mrs. Reed said. "Hold on a minute while I call Tina. She's playing with her dolls in the backyard."

It took just a few minutes before Erin heard a door bang and Tina squeal, "The zoo? Erin's going to take me to the zoo?" She snatched up the phone with more banging and clattering and shouted, "Erin! Are you really going to take me to the zoo?"

Erin smiled at the delight in Tina's voice. "That's right," she said. "And we'll wear disguises."

"Disguises? Like camels? Oh! I'll practice and see how far I can spit!"

"These will be *real* disguises," Erin told her. "You'll be a little girl, but you'll look very different, and we'll have a lot of fun."

"Just the two of us? Just you and me and nobody else? Promise?"

"Promise. Just you and me, except for your mother, but she said she wouldn't stay with us."

"Like when she's on the set."

"That's right."

Tina sighed with happiness and went on chatting until Erin heard Tina's mother remind her that the conversation was taking too long. "What if one of the studios wants to reach you and the line is busy?" she asked.

"I have to go now," Tina said, repeating her mother's instructions.

"I'll see you tomorrow," Erin said.

"I'm glad," Tina said. She paused. "Once I had a dream about you, and it made me cry because I miss you."

"I miss you, too," Erin said.

"You're still my sister," Tina told her.

"That's right."

"Mommie says I have to say good-bye."

"Good-bye," Erin said. She hung up the phone and stared at it. Wasn't it the same? While she'd been waiting for Lydia and Gene to call, Tina had been waiting for her, but she'd been too miserable with her own feelings to think about Tina's needs.

"I'm not going to feel guilty," Erin mumbled aloud. "Tina and I are going to the zoo and have a wonderful time together."

She groaned and buried her face in her arms.

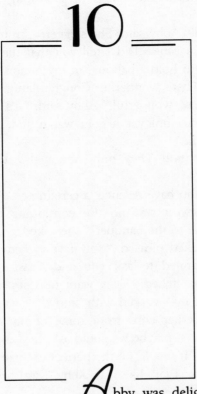

# 10

*A*bby was delighted to help plan the disguises. "You're right," she said. "Dress like two dirty, happy children, and no one will notice you." She rummaged through an old trunk in her wardrobe room until she found a faded cotton print dress and held it up. "I wore this in *Angel Babies,* when I tap-danced with Rusty Drew," she said. "Oh, how that man could dance!" She smiled. "Do you think this dress would fit Tina?"

"Abby!" Erin said. "This dress belongs in the Hollywood Museum!"

"So do I," Abby said. She staggered around like an old woman with a cane. "Did I tell you that the Film Association is going to hold a banquet in my honor in May?"

"Abby! That's wonderful! Congratulations!"

"It's not so wonderful," Abby said. "It's the equivalent of handing an employee a gold watch and saying 'Have a nice retirement.' "

"No, it's not! They only honor the most important stars."

"Ones who have reached 'a certain age.' "

Erin knew it was no use continuing the argument. "Could I come to the banquet?" she asked.

Abby looked pleased. "You *have* to come. As a matter of fact, I planned to ask you and Cassie to give short speeches." She sighed. "They want testimonials from some of the people I've worked with, and they want me to help them put together clips from some of my old films and television shows. Maybe we could ask for a copy and play it at my funeral. It would be the perfect obituary."

"Please don't talk like that, Abby," Erin begged. "They're honoring you."

"By dwelling on the past. I'd rather have a program about what I'll be doing in the future—if I still have a future in Hollywood."

"Of course you have a future," Erin began. "So you had a setback. You've had them before and come through. Before you know it, you'll—"

Abby interrupted. "Let's get back to the dress," she

said. "At this moment, you and Tina need the dress more than the Hollywood Museum does. Besides, when you return it we'll just wash it and tuck it back in the chest, and no one will know the difference."

"It might be a little big for Tina." Erin held the dress gingerly, remembering the film that she'd seen over and over again on video. "And honestly, Abby, I'm kind of scared to touch it."

"Well, don't be. Would it fit if we put some safety pins in it?"

Erin smiled. "I can make it fit."

"What are you going to wear? Do you have the right clothes?"

"I've got an old plaid blouse. One sleeve is torn, and it's faded. I'll wash it so it will be wrinkled, and I'll wear it with some khaki shorts."

"Also wrinkled," Abby reminded. "And it won't hurt if they don't look too clean." She struggled to her feet and gently put down the lid of the trunk. Moving to some mirror-covered doors, she opened one and searched through some round, patent-leather hatboxes until she found what she was looking for.

"Dark wigs," she said, smiling as she held one up against her own hair. "I wore this one, trying to disguise myself, when I was traveling on the *QE2* across the Atlantic." She shrugged. "It didn't work."

"What did you do to change your face?" Erin asked.

Abby's eyes widened. "What *could* I do? You don't think I'd be seen in public without my makeup, do you?"

"Some disguise!" Erin laughed at her grandmother and

began to tease her. "You wanted to be recognized, didn't you? You wanted to have people fall all over themselves to get near you and beg for your autograph."

Abby had to smile. "It's proof, baby, that you've still got it."

"Well, today I've got to hide Tina and myself under real disguises, or we'll never be able to go anywhere together again."

Abby pulled out a metal box the size of a traveling case. "Here's the makeup you'll need. I'd suggest reshaping your noses. That's the best way to give yourselves different faces. Here . . . I'll show you how to do it."

An hour later, Erin parked on the drive in front of her house and jumped out of the car. She was going to give her parents a laugh when they saw her in the wig, a broad, hump-shaped nose, and dirt-streaked makeup. She was close to the door when she realized that someone was lurking in the darkness near the front steps. She stopped short and raised the metal makeup case as though it were a weapon. "Get out of here!" she warned. "I'm going to yell!"

The figure stood up. "I'm the one who ought to yell," a familiar voice said. "What a mess! You really let yourself go, didn't you?"

"Eddie?" Forgetting her anger, Erin ran to him and hugged him. "Don't kiss me yet," she said. "I have to take my nose off first."

"You have a knack for making yourself undesirable," he murmured against her hair. "How come your hair smells like mothballs?" He stood back. "How come it isn't your own hair?"

"I've been practicing with disguises. I'm taking Tina to the zoo tomorrow morning, and we don't want anyone to recognize us."

Eddie smiled. "I like that," he said. "Can I come, too?"

Erin frowned. More than anything, she wished Eddie could come. "I don't think you'd better," she said. "I promised Tina it would be just the two of us."

"You mean Tina's mother is really going to let Tina out of her sight?"

"Not exactly. She'll come along, but she said she'd keep her distance."

"Some fun. You, Tina, and Mrs. Reed."

"I can put up with Mrs. Reed," Erin said. "Tina needed to know that I hadn't forgotten her."

"I need to know that, too," Eddie said.

Erin was glad the stage makeup covered her blushing. "Why didn't you call me?" she asked.

"I was waiting for you to cool down and call me."

"I thought you'd be in your Big Sur country. Were you here in town all along?"

"Not exactly," Eddie said. "I just got back a few days ago from the Big Sur."

"And you're complaining that I didn't call you? Who do you think you are?"

"Hey," Eddie said softly, "I missed you. All the time I was up north, I kept wishing you were with me. I wished I could share it all with you."

Erin's gaze dropped as her cheeks grew hot. "Don't think like that, Eddie," she said. "We're friends, and we want to stay friends."

He lifted her chin, and when she looked up at him, he said, "I wanted you to hear the forest coming alive in the morning. I wanted you to see how great it looks when the mist creeps from the sea up over the cliffs. I guess I wanted to watch how happy and surprised you'd look when you were surrounded by all that beauty. What kind of clod would I be if I wanted you there only to share a sleeping bag?"

Erin gulped. "I guess I'm the clod. For misunderstanding."

Eddie shrugged. "It's not your fault. All you've ever known is Hollywood." He smiled at Erin. "How does the old line go? 'Let me take you away from all this'?"

Erin smiled back at him. "Come on inside," she said. "I'll show my disguise to my parents, and then I'll take it off and wash my face." She ran up the steps and unlocked the front door. "Come on," she repeated.

As Eddie climbed the steps, she took his hand. "By the way, why were you sitting on our front porch?"

"I telephoned, and your father said you were expected back in about an hour, so I tried to time it. When I saw that your car wasn't here, I just sat down to wait."

"You could have gone inside and talked to Mom and Dad."

"Talking to parents makes me very uncomfortable," Eddie said. "They say things like, 'Are you planning to go to college?' and 'What does your father do for a living?' and stuff like that, and they expect sensible answers."

"My parents aren't going to ask you anything like that," Erin said with a laugh.

As she led Eddie into the den, her parents stared. Her

father stumbled to his feet and her mother dropped her newspaper and asked, "Erin! What happened to your nose?" She turned her wide-eyed gaze to Eddie.

"It's not my fault," Eddie said.

"This conversation sounds familiar." Erin laughed and explained about the trip to the zoo. "It was this, or paper bags over our heads," she said.

"Erin, doesn't this prove to you that you'd be much happier if you were free to do the things you like without having to go through all this subterfuge?" Cassie asked.

"Mom," Erin said, "please don't get started on this again."

"I'm not even sure your disguises will work. I'm concerned about what might happen if people discover who you and Tina are."

"We'll be all right!" Erin sighed, and rolled her eyes, not wanting to admit that she was a little scared, too, when she let herself think about the possibilities. For the past four years, she rarely went to public places, and then only to "safe" ones, like the Polo Lounge, whose customers were primarily people in the industry. She'd never forget those horrible people in the parking lot. What if people like that were visiting the zoo, which was a real draw for tourists? She shoved the thought from her mind and said, "We're going in the morning, before the zoo gets crowded, and Mrs. Reed will be there."

"How much help could Mrs. Reed be?"

"Mom, if this trip to the zoo is okay with Mrs. Reed, it ought to be okay with you. You know how protective she is. I *promised* Tina. You don't want me to go back on my promise, do you?"

"Well, no," Cassie said, "but I think we need to discuss this a little more."

"There's nothing to discuss." Erin's voice rose. "I told Tina I'd take her to the zoo. Are you going to tell me I can't?"

"Uh, maybe I better leave," Eddie said, but no one answered him. Erin just grasped his hand and held it tightly.

Marc put an arm around Cassie's shoulders, hugging her to him. "Calm down, Erin. Your mother is only trying to look after your best interests. It might have been a good idea to have checked this plan with her before you committed yourself to it."

Erin took a long breath and tried to speak calmly. Losing her temper wouldn't help. It never had before. "Maybe I should have asked Mom," she said to her father, "but I'm used to using my own judgment and not having to ask Mom what I can do, because Mom's not usually around to ask."

"I'll just see myself out." Eddie tried to pull his hand away from Erin's, but she didn't let go.

"Don't exaggerate, Erin." Cassie's voice was low and clipped, and Erin could see the hurt and surprise in her mother's eyes.

But Erin was hurt, too, and she stood without moving or speaking, stubbornly refusing to try to ease the situation.

Finally, her parents gave each other the kind of look that meant they were communicating without words—a look that Erin had always hated because it shut her out completely—and Cassie said, "All right, Erin. You've made the decision, so we'll let it stand."

"But next time you try something so unusual, we want you to check it out with us," Marc emphasized. "Got it?"

"I've got it," Erin mumbled.

"Then relax. Don't look so glum," her father teased. "I'll give you something happier to think about. In a few days, I may have a nice surprise for you and your mother."

"What is it?" Cassie asked.

Marc laughed. "I said it was a surprise. You'll have to be patient."

Erin turned to Eddie and said, "Wait here. I'll be right back."

As she ran off to her room to clean the putty and makeup from her face, she heard her father ask, "Well, Eddie, are you planning to go to college?"

When Erin rang the Reeds' doorbell, Tina stared at her suspiciously from behind her mother's legs.

"Shhhh," Erin said, bending to Tina's level. "I'm in disguise." She straightened and said, "I told you I'd disguise us so our fans wouldn't recognize us."

"Well, you certainly did that," Mrs. Reed said. She opened the door wider so that Erin could enter an entry hall that was cluttered with ornate sconces, tables, and mirrors. A heavy table was filled with gilt-framed photos of Tina, the frames overshadowing the little girl in the pictures.

As Erin shifted the beige canvas bag holding the things Tina would need, Tina tugged at it. "Do me!" she shouted.

It took less than fifteen minutes to turn Tina's delicate little nose into a rounder, pug nose and cover her face and neck with a darker makeup. She piled Tina's hair on top of her head, adjusted the wig over it, and anchored it with a few bobby pins. The ragged bangs fell over Tina's eyes, and she grinned at herself in the mirror.

"I can hardly believe what you've accomplished," Mrs. Reed told Erin. "We should get some posed glossies made. It could open up a whole new field for Tina if she weren't limited to roles calling for pretty little blondes."

Erin reached into the bag for the child's dress, which was folded on the bottom. She slipped the dress over Tina's head and arms and nipped in the waist and neck with two safety pins. "You look just right," she told Tina.

"When can we go?" Tina begged, jerking at Erin's arm as she tugged on it and jumped up and down.

"Right now," Erin said.

She drove through Hollywood and onto Los Feliz Boulevard, following the southern boundary of Griffith Park until she approached the Golden State Freeway and the road that led into the zoo area of the park.

As they left the parking lot and walked toward the entrance gates, Mrs. Reed hung back, allowing Erin and Tina to go ahead. Tina, so excited she was unable to walk without jumping and skipping, held Erin's hand tightly, releasing it only as Erin fished some bills out of her pocket and paid the admission charge.

There were already quite a few families enjoying the zoo. Many of them had cameras and were taking pictures of their children and of the animals. But a number of people without children were also on hand. A heavyset man with two cameras slung about his neck glanced speculatively at Erin and Tina, then at Mrs. Reed. For an instant, Erin held her breath. Had he recognized them? But the man soon seemed to lose interest and his glance slid away.

As they entered the zoo area, an odd man wearing an old leather jacket and a cap, which was pulled over his ears in spite of the warm day, roughly brushed against her.

"Watch it!" Erin said as she stumbled and caught her balance, but he stomped along the path, ignoring her as though she weren't there.

*Well, that's what I want, isn't it—to be ignored?* Erin thought. "Come on," she said to Tina, leading her around a pair of surveyors who were sighting and measuring and making notations in a notebook. "Let's see the elephants first."

The girls ate popcorn and ice cream and drank sodas and imitated the monkeys, and all the while Mrs. Reed followed at a distance.

But the man with the cameras appeared to be following them, too. He'd been standing near the entrance when they'd arrived, and he'd chosen the route they'd taken. Each time Erin had turned to study the man, he'd been adjusting the telephoto lenses on one of his cameras or sighting an animal through a viewfinder, yet she had the uncomfortable feeling that he'd been photographing her—or Tina—when she wasn't aware.

The guy in the leather jacket moved past them, and Erin realized that she'd seen a lot of him this morning, too. He didn't seem to have a plan or purpose. Erin nervously thought of stories she'd heard about obsessed fans stalking young actresses. All alone, the man wandered up the path, then back down again, often skirting the engineers, who seemed to be surveying the entire zoo. She tried to get a good look at his face, but his collar was up, his cap was low on his forehead, and all she could glimpse was a bit of blotchy skin and a scraggly, dirty, blond mustache.

It was nearly noon when a deep voice spoke directly behind Erin, so close that she jumped. She whirled to face the man with the cameras. His forehead was beaded with sweat and was red from the sun, and he ran the back of his hand across it.

"Hey, girls," he said again. "I'm doing a picture story on the zoo, and I need a couple of close-ups of kids smiling directly at the camera. How about the two of you posing for me?"

"No, thanks," Erin said, but he'd already snapped one close-up picture and was circling to get a better view of Tina. He aimed again, but paused and glanced at Erin. "Fix her wig," he said. "It's lopsided."

"What? Who are you?" Erin cried. She grabbed Tina and stood protectively in front of her.

"Hey, look, it's okay. So I blew it. Just fix her wig, let's get a couple of shots, and we'll be through."

Erin grabbed for the camera the man was holding and tried to twist it out of his hands. "Oh, no you don't!" she yelled, but he shoved her away with such force that she landed on the ground.

"Tina!" Erin screamed. "Run to your mother! Run!"

Tina burst into loud wails and clung to Erin.

As Erin struggled to her feet, she saw Mrs. Reed racing toward them, one hand holding her hat, which was flopping wildly. "It's all right, Erin! Don't shout! It's all right!" Mrs. Reed called.

Others ran toward them, too. The young man in the jacket made a flying leap at the photographer's back, wrapped him in a headlock, and hung on tightly, even though the man was much stronger and was shaking him violently. A blond mustache flew through the air and landed at Erin's feet.

"I'll hold him! Get out of here, Erin!" the young man shouted.

"Eddie?" Erin yelled.

But the fracas was over as fast as it had begun. Erin was pushed back by one of the two surveyors, who gripped the photographer's arms, twisting them behind his back.

"Hey, look! I was hired for this job!" the photographer complained. "Just ask Mrs. Reed."

Mrs. Reed, whose face was flushed with embarrassment, fanned herself with her hat. "Erin, he's from *Hollywood Photo*. This could be great publicity for Tina. For you, too," she said quickly.

"We were supposed to be here just to have fun together," Erin said.

"But you have had fun, haven't you?"

The surveyor who was holding the photographer let go of his arms, handed him his camera, and motioned toward the zoo exit. Without a word, the photographer scrambled to get out of the way, brushing himself off as he loped for the gate.

"You father said to take care of you," the surveyor told

Erin. He nodded toward the crowd that had gathered. "With all these people here, it looks as though you'd better leave right now."

"My father sent you?" Furious, Erin marched toward the exit, the others following.

When they got to the parking lot, Erin turned to the pseudosurveyors. "Are you from the studio?" she asked.

"Yes, ma'am," one of them said.

"Do you have room in your car to take Mrs. Reed and Tina home?"

"Sure," the other said.

Erin bent to hug Tina good-bye. "We did have fun for a while," she said, "and I'll come and see you again. Don't cry."

As Mrs. Reed climbed into the studio's car, Erin complained to Eddie, "We could have had a wonderful time, except for Mrs. Reed. She makes me so mad!"

Eddie peeled off his leather jacket and cap. "Can you give me a ride?" he asked Erin. "I hitched a lift on the back of a friend's Harley to get here."

Startled by the change of subject, Erin took a few moments to react. "What happened to your car?" she asked.

"I didn't want you to see it and recognize it."

Erin fished her car keys from the pocket of her shorts but paused before she opened the car doors. "I thought you were going to buy a Bronco."

"That was when I thought I had a guaranteed income for next season. Who knows how long it will be between jobs? The Bronco can come after I've got another job nailed down."

As they drove back toward Los Feliz Boulevard, Erin couldn't help reliving the experience in the zoo. "You weren't supposed to be there," Erin told Eddie. "Why did you come?"

"I got to thinking about what your parents told you," Eddie said. "I guess they were right."

"No, they weren't!" Erin gave him a furious look, then turned back to watching the traffic. "None of us knew what Mrs. Reed would do. I still can't believe she'd pull a trick like that!"

"Well, you should believe it," Eddie said. "And you should believe what your mother told you, too. If it weren't for your father lining up those two guys and alerting zoo security . . ."

"He alerted the zoo?" Erin was even more indignant. She found that she was speeding and eased the pressure on the accelerator. "It's not fair!" she muttered. "I could have pulled it off, and without any help!"

"I don't think so," Eddie said quietly.

"What do you know about it?" Erin shouted.

"I know better than to try to live in two different worlds at once. And I know enough to separate the make-believe world from the real world, which is something you're going to have to learn to do."

"Acting is *not* a make-believe world. It's my life!"

"You don't understand what I mean, Erin."

"No! *You* don't understand!"

They had reached the stoplight at Franklin Avenue, where Los Feliz curved into Western Avenue. Eddie suddenly opened the door on the passenger side of the car.

---

"Thanks for the ride," he said, scooping up his jacket and cap. "I can take the bus from here."

Before Erin could answer, he'd closed the door and had sprinted across the street.

In her frustration, she punched at the wrong buttons to open her car window. By the time she'd finally managed to open it, Eddie was striding down the sidewalk on the opposite side of the street, too far away to hear her.

She could still picture Eddie as he hung on the back of the photographer, trying his best to help her. "I didn't thank him," she said with a groan. "I didn't even remember to thank him."

Erin made a right turn on Franklin Avenue and headed for home. She was so angry—and so alone.

## 11

$\mathcal{E}$rin wasn't sure which was worse—being tricked out of the day of fun with Tina or having to tell her parents the story. If her mother had just once said, "I told you so," Erin knew she would have exploded. But Cassie didn't. She listened to what Erin had to say without asking even one question, then sat there thinking.

It was the silent thinking that bothered Erin the most.

What was her mother thinking about? Whatever it was, Erin knew she wasn't going to like it.

She'd escape to Abby's house.

No—then she'd have to go through the whole story again. Erin trudged up the stairs to her room, cleaned off her makeup, and climbed into a hot bath, where she sank to her chin, scowling at the bubbles that floated on top of the water.

It was later, as she lay across her bed, wondering if she could call Eddie and apologize without starting to blubber, that the telephone rang.

She didn't reach for it. She even hoped it wouldn't be for her. But her mother's voice floated up the stairs. "Erin! Telephone!"

Erin unwillingly picked up the receiver and answered.

"Hi, little babe," a voice said, "it's me. Jake."

Erin climbed to her knees and sat up. "Jake?"

"Yeah. I bet you've been wondering and wondering if I meant it when I said I'll call you."

"Not so anyone would notice," Erin answered. Jake and his big ego! His good looks weren't worth it.

Jake chuckled, obviously not believing her. "It's party time," he said. "Tonight."

"What party?"

"At Johnny Rapp's—from *Street Cop*." Erin knew who Johnny was. He played Stash, a young hood. "It should be fun, and a lot of the people on his show are going to be there, including the producer. My agent told me it would be good for me to show up, so I'm going, and I thought about you. You said you liked to party."

"What about Marcie?"

"What about her? She dropped me for some guy on the set of that film she's making. Big deal. There was nothing serious between us. Listen, do you want to go or not? If you don't, I've got to line up another date."

*Why not go?* Erin thought. Anything was better than staying home tonight. She began to answer, but remembered her father's admonition. Grimacing, she said, "Give me your phone number, Jake. I'll have to check it out and let you know."

"No problem," he said, and recited the number, adding, "Call me back as soon as you can. Okay?"

Erin walked downstairs and found her mother in the den, where she was curled in a chair, so lost in a book that she didn't hear Erin come in. She jumped when Erin said, "Mom!"

"Sorry," Cassie said. She held up the book so Erin could see it. It was Lydia's copy of *The Dorchesters.* "This is a terrific story. I saw the book on the upstairs hall table and borrowed it. I hope you don't mind."

"I don't mind." Still in her bad mood and wanting to make herself even more miserable, Erin said, "Orion or somebody wants to option it, and Marcie's pretty sure she's going to get the part of Kim."

"That's odd," Cassie said. "Marcie strikes me as being the wrong type for Kim. Marcie's too much the Hollywood-starlet type."

"Mom," Erin said, "Jake invited me to go to a party tonight." She told Cassie where the party would be. "So is it okay? Will you let me go?"

"Do you know any of those people?" Cassie asked.

"I know Jake."

"Do you know much about him?"

"I know he's not as dumb as the character he plays—played—on *The Family Next Door*. He's awfully conceited, but other than that, he's all right."

"How old is Jake?"

"Eighteen."

Cassie thought a moment. "Honey, I'd rather you were dating boys who aren't actors, nice normal kids you'd meet through your school friends."

Erin groaned. "Mom, get real."

"You're right," Cassie said, which surprised Erin. "Okay. It's *this* party we're dealing with, not one I'd like you to go to." She paused before she said, "You're sensible enough to get out of a bad situation, Erin, and I trust you. If you see anyone using drugs, or if any of the young people are drinking—"

"I know. I'll call you and Dad and take a taxi home." She edged toward the door.

Cassie sighed. "Could we wait until Marc gets home and ask him before you call Jake back?"

"No," Erin said. "Jake has to know right away, because if I can't come, he'll ask somebody else."

"Do you really want to go?"

Up until this moment, Erin really hadn't cared, but now the party seemed very important. "Yes," she said. "I do."

"All right," Cassie told her. "But we want to meet Jake when he picks you up. Make sure he understands that."

Erin ran all the way upstairs to call Jake, unwilling to use the phones downstairs, where someone might overhear her conversation.

Judging from the noise level on the street in front of Johnny Rapp's apartment, the party was well underway as Erin and Jake arrived.

"It pays to be late," Jake explained, raising his voice above the music, which Erin recognized as the Fine Young Cannibals. "That way you don't look too eager. Also, you can scout out who's there and go right for the important people who can do you some good."

Erin winced, but Jake didn't seem to notice. He took her hand and led her into the apartment-house lobby as he said, "We'll both make a few points tonight. Like you having a date with me, which a lot of girls would die for; and me being with you because you're related to Abby Grant. I mean, it makes people notice and talk, and that's all to the good."

Erin pulled her hand away. "That's the reason you asked me? Because of Abby?"

"Naw," he said, and recaptured her hand, pulling her toward the stairs. "I told you, you're growing up. You're a good-looking girl, Erin. I was just spelling out the business side."

A small, elderly woman opened her door just enough to poke her head out. With one hand she clutched the neckline of a cotton print robe together and pleaded, "If those are your friends upstairs making all that racket, please ask them to turn down the music. It's nearly ten o'clock, and how anybody's going to sleep through all that din, I don't know."

Erin tried to look sympathetic, and shrugged as they passed the woman.

The noise was even louder as they squeezed past a few people who were seated on the steps, drinks in their hands. Each woman looked up at Erin as though she were judging the competition, then looked away, satisfied. Erin would have liked to have stepped on a few fingers or toes. She was wearing a lavender-blue silk blouse and matching skirt that flowed like a cloud around her legs, and she knew she looked good.

The door to the apartment had been left open, so they entered without ceremony. Jake immediately made a beeline to a pudgy man with wisps of curly black hair dotting his scalp as though they'd been planted with the hope that they'd grow and spread. Poor thing, Erin thought. He had more hair on his chest, which showed through the gap in his unbuttoned shirt.

The man perked up and smiled as he saw Erin, and she heard the words "Willie" and "producer," and part of what she assumed was the name of his production company. She wished he wouldn't stare at her so intently. She felt his eyes on her as she followed Jake around the room, smiling and nodding and wondering what in the world was being said. The music was good, but she agreed with the woman downstairs that it was much too loud. Her head was starting to hurt.

She munched on some celery and dip and pizza wedges, which were beginning to dry and curl on the edges, and sipped on a Coke. Jake had disappeared into the crowd, and Erin didn't care. She wished she hadn't come with him. The jerk! Inviting her because she was Abby Grant's grand-daughter! This was a rotten party, and the sooner she could leave, the better it would be.

Someone staggered in with a large, heavy tray of small quiches and plopped it down on the side of the table in front of Erin.

Just as she'd filled her mouth with a large bite of quiche, the producer named Willie appeared at her side, mouthed something she was unable to understand, and finally took her shoulders and steered her out of the apartment and onto the landing.

"It's impossible to hear each other in there," he said, "and I want to talk to you. Let's walk down to the end of the hall. I see there's an open window down there."

As they reached the window, Erin gratefully took a couple of deep breaths of the cool air.

"My compliments and condolences," Willie said. He scratched at one of his tufts of hair and added, "Compliments on your excellent work on *The Family Next Door*, and condolences because it's over. It's tough to be on top one minute and out of work the next."

"That's what I've discovered," Erin said, and tried a smile to lighten her words.

"So . . . what has your agent got lined up for you?"

"There was going to be a commercial," Erin said, "but the company's involved in some kind of takeover, so the commercial was put on hold."

He nodded sympathetically. "How'd you like to be in a

major film? Big budget—over twenty million—and it's going to get rave reviews, I guarantee."

"I'd love to be in a film!" Erin stood up a little straighter.

"We've just started working on the casting, so fortunately the teenaged-daughter role hasn't been filled. It's a big part and a strong one, and you'd be perfect for it."

Erin found it hard to breathe. "T-thank you," she mumbled.

Willie fished a business card from a shiny brass card holder in the pocket of his slacks and handed it to her. "Give me your agent's name, and I'll get in touch with him on Monday. You'll have to audition, of course, but as far as I'm concerned, the part is yours."

"My agent is Zack Fremont," she said.

Willie smiled and held up two crossed fingers. "Zack and I are like that. I worked with his father, too. Good men, both of them."

Erin could hardly believe what was happening. She'd just been offered a part in a film! "Tell me about the story," she said. "What is it? Contemporary? Adventure?"

"Comedy," he said. "We're talking a big-name star for the lead, but haven't got a commitment yet, so I can't come out and say who it is." He paused and winked. "Did you happen to see *Dead Poets' Society*?"

"Robin Williams? Really?"

"I said I can't say, and nothing's on paper. You understand how these things can change until it's all in writing."

Erin put her fingertips to her cheeks. "Of course," she said. "Wow! I can't believe all this!"

He shrugged. "Sometimes it happens like that. You've

got what I've been looking for—the sweet, innocent expression that's completely opposite from the sexually aggressive character you'll play."

Erin wasn't sure she'd heard him right. "What kind of character?"

"It's a great part—a kid going all out after her mother's boyfriend. You don't have any problem with doing nude scenes, do you?"

Erin's hands dropped to her sides, and she stared at him. "Nude scenes? You mean me? Nude?"

"That's right. It's a wacko script, and those scenes are some of the funniest."

"I—I can't do nude scenes," Erin said, her face burning with embarrassment.

Willie smiled and reached out a pudgy hand to pat her shoulder. "Actresses are always a little nervous the first time. Well, don't worry. We'll close the set to everyone except the cast and crew. Only a handful of people will see you."

"How about all the people who'll go to see the movie, or who'll rent videos of the film, or watch it on cable!"

"Don't make up your mind right now," he said. "Give my offer some thought, and I'll talk to Zack first thing Monday morning. Remember, this is going to be a major film, and it could be a once-in-a-lifetime opportunity for you."

"I—I've got to find Jake," Erin stammered, and ran down the hall and back into the room. All she wanted to do was go home.

She had squirmed her way into the kitchen, shielding her ears against the deafening beat of the Falsely Accused, when the music was suddenly turned off. People began yelling in the front room. Then two uniformed policemen burst into the kitchen. One shoved Erin against the wall, and one of them shouted at a couple near the sink, warning them not to move. Erin saw the drug paraphernalia at the same time she heard a voice in the living room order, "Take them all in."

"But I didn't know anyone was using drugs," Erin had told her father and mother over and over again after they'd come to the Beverly Hills police station to pick her up. "And I wasn't arrested!"

Cassie couldn't hide her irritation. She flopped into one of the big chairs in the den and frowned at Erin. "You shouldn't have had to be taken to the police station in the first place. We trusted you to use your common sense and come home if there was anything going on that shouldn't have been. The police said that a number of people had been drinking," she added.

Erin shrugged. "So? People are drinking at your parties, and Abby's parties, and our cast parties."

"But not people who are underage."

"I didn't go around asking how old everybody was!"

"Don't shout, Erin," Marc said. "We're trying to sort all this out and help you."

"I don't want to talk about it anymore!" Erin said.

"All right," her mother said. "We won't talk about it, except for giving you our decision."

"What decision?" Erin immediately became suspicious.

"For one thing," her father said, "no more parties unless they're with people we know and approve of."

Erin shrugged. That wasn't so bad. She not only wasn't likely to be invited to any more parties, but she had no desire to go to any more like this disastrous one that had gotten her into so much trouble.

It dawned on her that her father had said "for *one* thing." There had to be something else. Erin looked at her mother.

"Erin, honey," Cassie said, "we made a mistake in letting you go for an acting career at such a young age. You've missed so much of your childhood. You don't have any girlfriends your age, and while other kids have been out having fun with their school friends, you've been working."

"But I like—"

"My turn," Cassie said firmly. "Just listen." As Erin nodded reluctantly, Cassie said, "Marc and I allowed you to make a pilot for *The Family Next Door* because we were so sure you'd decide on your own that it wasn't something you really wanted. But our permissiveness backfired. You loved everything about it."

"Of course I did! I do!"

"If you want an acting career, you can make that choice when you're grown. On Monday, I'm going to enroll you in Windsor Academy for your last year of high school."

"No!" Erin exploded. "That's not fair! You're forcing your own idea of what life should be on me." She was so upset that it was hard not to cry, but she kept back the tears.

When she cried, she lost, and she had to convince her parents that they were wrong.

For an instant, she could see a flicker of hesitation in her father's eyes, so she zeroed in on him. "When you were young, I bet you chose what you wanted to do." She glanced at her mother. "How about you, Mom? I know you didn't want to be just exactly like your own mother. You wanted to plan your own life."

Cassie blushed, and looked away, and Erin knew she'd made a point. "Mom and I are very different," Erin said to Marc. "Just because *she* went to Windsor doesn't mean I should go. Just because *she* wasn't interested in acting doesn't mean I shouldn't be. Don't you understand?"

"Well, uh, I guess we can see your viewpoint," Marc said. He rubbed at his bearded chin and looked to Cassie for help.

"You should know that I don't want you to be a carbon copy of me," Cassie told Erin. "I love you for yourself."

"You love me if I do what *you* want me to do."

"That's not true."

"That's the way I see it."

Cassie let out a long sigh. "All right, Erin. If there's another school you'd rather go to, we can talk about it. If—"

"I was offered a part in a film tonight," Erin said. "It's a big-budget film, with major stars. The producer's going to talk to Zack." She fished Willie's card out of her pocket and handed it to her mother, who looked at it and gave it to Marc.

He nodded. "I know his work. He's got good credits."

"Okay," Erin said, beginning to relax. "I'm not going to take the part, but the offer should prove to you that people in the business are aware of me, that I've got a chance for more work, and that the end of *The Family Next Door* doesn't mean the end of my career."

Again, Marc looked at Cassie. "Maybe if we talk this over some more—"

But Cassie had caught Erin's first statement, and she said, "What do you mean that you're not going to take the part?"

"I mean that I wouldn't want it."

"Why not, Erin? What's wrong with it?"

Erin gulped, squeezed her eyes shut for a second, and hoped that what she had to tell them wouldn't ruin everything. "Because the part calls for nude scenes."

"Nude scenes! Not our daughter!" Cassie cried, while Marc muttered something under his breath.

"Weren't you listening to me?" Erin insisted. "I told you I didn't want the part."

Cassie angrily tore Willie's business card in two and threw the pieces on the floor. "We can make sure that you won't be subjected to offers like that again!"

"Mom!" Erin shouted, terrified at what her mother had just said. "Good parts in good movies will come up! Or in television! What about those?"

To Erin's horror, Cassie shook her head firmly and said, "Those are all 'ifs,' Erin. You need to come down to earth. There's not a doubt in my mind now that Marc and I have made the right decision."

# 12

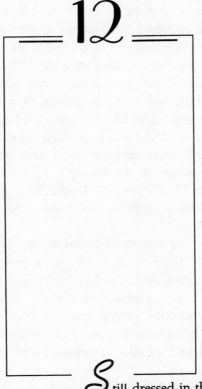

$\mathcal{S}$till dressed in the T-shirt she had worn to bed, Erin sat in her room the next morning, not wanting to come out. Her stomach growled with hunger, but she'd rather skip breakfast than have to talk to her mother. She could have won over her father, she was sure. He'd been ready to give in. It was her mother who'd been the stubborn one.

Erin was furious with herself, too, for having brought up the movie offer.

"I only wanted to prove that my career didn't have to be over," she muttered. She kicked at the flowered quilt that trailed in a clump over the edge of the bed and managed to bang her heel against a leg of the bed. As she rubbed the painful spot, tears came to her eyes.

Sitting there wallowing in misery didn't help. She'd have to do something to take her mind off her parents and off her empty stomach, which growled again. Erin looked around her self-imposed prison and saw only the book she'd already read—*The Dorchesters*.

Marcie in *The Dorchesters*. Damn! Why did it have to be Marcie? With a swipe of one hand, Erin knocked the book to the floor.

She knew her parents had been wrong. There *would* be other job offers. *Good* offers. She'd done a great job with her television character, and it would lead to other TV shows. Maybe movie roles. Marcie had done it. Her career had suddenly skyrocketed. So why couldn't Erin's? If she were offered a part her mother'd approve of, she'd have to change her mind and let Erin take it, wouldn't she? Of course she would.

Willie had said he'd talk to Zack first thing Monday morning, but Erin wanted to talk to Zack first. It was Saturday, and Zack wouldn't be at his office. If she telephoned him at home, he'd probably want to kill her.

The way she felt, that didn't matter. She looked up Zack's home telephone number in her address book and dialed the phone.

Zack wasn't in bed. He was outside by his pool—Erin could hear his children splashing and laughing—and his voice was hearty. Erin allowed herself a quick sigh of relief before she got right to the point and told him about Willie and his offer.

"Nice going!" Zack said.

"No. He told me I'd have to do nude scenes, so when he calls, turn it down," she said. "I'm not going to do nude scenes."

"If you want to be successful, you'll have to learn to jump at offers like this," Zack said.

But Erin interrupted. "That's not the way I want to go."

"I won't try to talk you into it," Zack said. "It's up to you. I just want you to think about some of the kids who didn't let a little nudity stand in their way, like Brooke Shields and—"

"No," Erin said.

"Okay, if that's what you want." Zack answered so readily that Erin realized he already had other clients in mind for the part. "Remember," he added, "if something that's right for you comes up, I'll call you."

Erin put down the phone and pulled on a pair of jeans and a blouse as fast as she could. There was just one person she wanted to be with right now, and that was Abby.

Abby was in the sun room with Bobby and Mary Lou, all of them sipping coffee and reading various sections of *The Los Angeles Times* and *The New York Times*.

"How is everything going, Erin?" Mary Lou asked.

Erin groaned. She poured herself some orange juice and buttered two blueberry muffins. Fortified, she gulped down the first muffin and said, "Mom wants me to go to Windsor Academy."

Abby tossed aside the sports section of the newspaper and looked at Erin sharply. "Windsor is one of the best. As you know, it's where your mother went to school."

"I didn't mean it wasn't a good school," Erin hurried to say. "I just don't want to go to a real school. I want to be signed for another TV show or a movie."

"Maybe your agent will come up with something." Mary Lou tried to sound hopeful.

"In this business, you don't sit around and hope for something to happen," Abby said. "You make it happen."

"Marcie gets offers," Erin complained. "Right now she's in the middle of filming a comedy called *Spyscraper,* and she thinks she may even get cast in *The Dorchesters.*"

Abby frowned. "She's all wrong for *The Dorchesters.* The granddaughter isn't a bimbo."

Erin grinned at her grandmother. "We think alike," she said.

"I've read *The Dorchesters,*" Mary Lou said. She leaned back in her lounger. "What a wonderful story! I broke down during that reconciliation scene and cried buckets. Oh! It makes me want to cry again, just thinking about it."

"I've heard talk about it at the studio," Bobby put in. "No one's actually optioned the book. For a while there was something about Spielberg doing it, I think, with Audrey Hepburn as the grandmother, but that fell through."

"I can't see Spielberg making that story," Abby said. "It's not his type of film. Ron Howard, maybe."

"And Audrey Hepburn would be all wrong," Mary Lou said. "The grandmother's rich as sin, but a lot more earthy than Audrey Hepburn could play it."

"Joanne Woodward?" Bobby suggested.

"No. What about Anne Bancroft?"

As the idea struck her Erin took a quick breath and stared at Abby. "You know who'd be perfect in that part?" she asked. When they all turned to look at her, she said, "You, Abby."

"Me? Impossible. Judith is hard and unyielding. She doesn't want to give an inch." She rolled her eyes. "There's no humor in the grandmother's part. Where would the comedy come from?"

Erin scrambled across the room to kneel next to Abby and held her hands. "There doesn't have to be comedy in it, Abby! You're a wonderful actress! That's what makes you such a good comic. And that's why you'd be terrific in a serious role."

"That's absurd," Abby said, her gaze still locked with Erin's.

"No, it isn't." Mary Lou put her empty cup and saucer on the coffee table, brushed some crumbs from her white skirt, and turned to face Abby. "I think Erin is making a lot of good sense."

"Oh, really?" Abby pulled her hands away from Erin and held them outstretched. "I can see the headlines in *Variety* now: *Flap Over Flop as Grant Flips*."

"That's wrong. It won't be a flop," Erin said. "Think

about it, Abby. It would be something new and exciting for you."

"That's what they said about my variety show, and look what happened." She made a thumbs-down gesture.

"But this is entirely different. You could prove to everyone what a great actress you are."

"You'd knock their socks off," Mary Lou said.

Abby had to laugh, but she shook her head. "Be serious," she told them. "The woman in *The Dorchesters* is at least twenty—well, maybe ten—years older than I am. They'd have to make me look older, probably with some awful latex wrinkles, and I'd feel naked without my makeup. I look *horrible* without my makeup, and I wouldn't want my fans to see me like that."

Mary Lou reached for one of Abby's hands. "I've heard that complaint before," she said, "when Cassie was just a couple of years older than Erin is now, and you were wrong."

"Oh," Abby said, her voice dropping. "You mean Cassie's photographs in *Coup*."

"What's *Coup*?" Erin asked.

"It was a big photo magazine," Mary Lou said. "It hasn't been around for years. *People* magazine killed it." She turned to Abby. "Remember the respect and the acclaim you got? Your fans saw the serious side of you, and they loved it."

Abby shrugged. "I felt very uncomfortable about those photographs."

"Not for long you didn't." Mary Lou smiled. "Your act didn't fool me for a second. When the reporters started calling, and the photographs were mentioned in every entertainment column in the United States, you ate it all up!"

"How would you know that?" Abby tried to look indignant but couldn't manage to hold back the laughter.

"Because I know you almost as well as I know myself."

"I guess you do," Abby admitted.

"And I know that you're trying to set up a thousand arguments against playing that role in *The Dorchesters*, because you're secretly a little scared that you can't pull it off."

"Now, just a minute," Abby began.

"But you can, so stop arguing and start thinking."

For a minute, Abby and Mary Lou sat silently, trying to outstare each other, until Abby broke away with a chuckle. "Do you really think I could do that part justice?" she asked.

"Of course I do."

"Oh, Abby, you know you can!" Erin gave an excited bounce.

Abby turned to her brother, who had been sitting quietly. "Bobby," she said, "you've always been one of my most truthful critics. What do you think?"

Bobby grinned. "I think you should go for it," he said.

Abby thought a moment. "Only if the right actress is cast as the granddaughter," she said.

Erin grimaced. "Please, don't say Marcie Lane," she mumbled.

"Not Marcie," Abby said firmly. "Erin Jenkins."

"What?" Erin dropped back on her heels, nearly losing her balance.

Mary Lou nodded as she stared at Erin. "That might work," she said slowly.

Bobby smiled enthusiastically. "What a team!" he said.

Erin shook her head. "I haven't got the big name. I'd be a nothing at the box office."

Abby gave an impatient wave of her hand. "*My* name will be the draw at the box office."

"Oh, I know that," Erin answered quickly, but she was still dubious about the role. "Kim is a major part, and whoever makes the film will want to cast it with someone who's well-known—not in television, but in films."

Abby cocked an eyebrow and said, "I see. You think you can't handle the part."

"I didn't say that!" Erin cried. "I could do a good job with the part! When I read the book, I could really identify with Kim, and mentally I was playing the role all through the story."

As Abby grinned, Erin had to laugh. "You tricked me," she said.

"I wanted to get your honest reaction."

Erin nodded. "Okay. You asked me once if I've got what it takes to make it all happen for me. And the answer is yes. I do."

"Then are we agreed?" Abby asked. "Could we make the film together?"

"Oh, yes!" Erin said. So filled with excitement that she couldn't contain it, she flung herself at her grandmother and wrapped her arms around her.

Abby began to laugh.

"What's so funny?" Erin asked.

"Us," Abby said. "We've just cast ourselves in a film no one plans to produce."

"Couldn't we produce it?" Erin asked.

Abby stopped laughing and looked at her. "Do you realize how much money it would take to produce that film?"

"Ten million, at least," Bobby interjected, and Mary Lou gasped.

Erin said, "But that's because of how much it would cost to pay the stars and the director. If you and I took the lead roles, Abby, we could take some kind of deferred salary, couldn't we? Or no salary and a percentage of the profits?"

"How do you know all that?" Mary Lou asked Erin.

"It's part of the business. Only the dumb actors don't read their contracts."

"Could you handle the financing yourself?" Bobby asked his sister.

Abby gave a rueful chuckle and held her arms wide. "All this costs a great deal to keep up, and as you know, during the last few years there hasn't been much coming in." She frowned as she thought. "If I liquidated my real-estate holdings and a few other investments, I'd still be able to come up with only a tenth of what we'd need, and if we lost our gamble . . . well, I'd be wiped out."

"No," Erin said. "We'll find another way."

Abby stood and walked slowly to the large glass windows that looked out on the garden. The reflection of its clipped green lawn and gleaming blue pool shimmered around her. "As just a part of the expense, there's studio rental, salaries for hairdressers, makeup artists, and crew, equipment rental, and lab costs. We just might line up an investor who'd be willing to gamble on a high percentage of the profits, but we'd have to pay an arm and a leg for a top director," she said. She turned to face the others. "As a rough estimate, I can't see bringing the film in for much less than five million. And then there's the problem of getting the right distribution. That can be chancy."

Mary Lou looked from Abby to Bobby to Erin. "Who are the people who invest in films?" she asked. "Can't we make a list of names and ask them?"

Abby smiled. "It's not quite that simple," she said.

"You know so many people in the television industry. Won't that help?"

"Right now, the television people consider me dead and buried," Abby said. "They all follow each other like sheep, so it would be hard to find a single person in this town who'd think my name would draw fans into a theater. That lets out the major studios."

"But it's not true that your career is over. You don't believe that, do you?"

"It's been a long time since I've made a movie, but what difference does it make—television or movies? I've still got the name recognition and the talent," Abby said. She sat a little taller, gaining confidence. "And I know there are plenty of fans out there who think I've got what it takes."

Erin persisted. "Okay, if we forget the major studios, who can we go to?"

"Well," Abby said, "there are the independent production companies like Orion and Lorimar. They often finance independent producers, but they're usually tied in with a major studio for production and distribution."

"Does that mean they wouldn't be interested either?"

Abby shrugged, and Mary Lou broke in. "What about one of those investment groups?"

"It's a possibility," Abby said. "But we'd need to have a complete package to show them: script, director, stars—the whole thing."

Bobby slowly stood up. "Abby," he said, "you'd really like to make this film. Am I right?"

"It's better than sitting around the house doing nothing," she said.

"That's not enough of an answer. Is this film something you'd really like to do? I need to know."

Abby nodded. "There's not much else left for me, is there? Sure, I'm scared, just as Mary Lou pointed out." She grimaced at Mary Lou, who gave a little, apologetic shrug. "But I've never in my life been really afraid to take risks, and I'm not now. To act in *The Dorchesters* with Erin . . . well, yes, I want to do it, Bobby. I want it a lot."

"Do you have enough money to option the book?" he asked.

Abby looked surprised. "With all this talk about production costs, I should have thought of the option. I guess we'll have to option it to keep someone else from getting it."

"Do you have enough?" he persisted.

She nodded. "Yes. That I can do."

Bobby nodded, his face serious. "Okay, then," he said. "If you can option the book, I'll start talking to some people about investing. I know a lot of people around this town, and I've got some good contacts."

As he left the room, Erin cringed, and felt the mood in the room sag a little. She could see the pity on Abby's face and knew they were thinking the same thing: Poor Bobby. His "contacts" existed only in his wishful thinking. If anything, when they made the movie, Abby would find a way to give Bobby some work on it. And they *would* make the movie.

Erin climbed to her feet, crossed the room, and gave her grandmother another hug. "Do me a favor, Abby," she pleaded. "Until it's all set, don't tell Mom and Dad. I want to surprise them."

They were going to be surprised, all right.

# 13

$\mathcal{I}$t was hard for Erin to sleep, and even harder for her to concentrate during the next few days. Without complaint, she dutifully went with Cassie to visit Windsor Academy, smiled sweetly at the headmistress, Penelope Keating, and arranged a date during the next week in which to take placement exams.

"Erin is a good student," her mother volunteered, nodding her head in emphasis.

Erin could see that her mother's knuckles were white as she gripped her handbag. *Why should she be so nervous? Does it mean that much to her?* Erin tried to hide her resentment, but she couldn't help thinking, *Why should I have to do everything the way Mom did it?*

Mrs. Keating pursed her thin lips and said with exaggerated patience, "We may find quite a difference between the quality of teaching to which Erin has been exposed and the high standards at Windsor Academy."

Erin wished she could tell the headmistress how wrong she was. Miss Blevins, her studio teacher, had been wonderful and warm and friendly, but had demanded the best work from her students. If there was going to be any comparison, Miss Blevins would come out way ahead!

Erin toured the campus with her mother and Mrs. Keating, whose gold-rimmed magnifying glass on a chain swung like a pendulum as she swayed down the walk. *Maybe she hypnotizes students with it,* Erin thought. *Back and forth, back and forth, you are in my power.* She suppressed a giggle, trying to look innocent as her mother shot a quick glance in her direction.

As a bell rang and students moved from one class to another, Erin and her mother received many appraisals from the girls, from quick side-glances to out-and-out stares. Erin stared right back at their navy-and-green-plaid skirts, white shirts, and navy blazers. Wasn't that what her mother had said she'd worn when she was here a million years ago?

It didn't matter. Erin could live through this day, because she knew she wouldn't be sent to Windsor next fall. If Abby could option *The Dorchesters,* surely the rest would fall into place.

Erin was so intent on her wishes that she was startled to find that the tour had ended and Mrs. Keating was saying, "I hope you realize, Erin, that it is only because your mother was a Windsor girl that you'll be a student here."

"Yes, I do," Erin said with such firmness that Cassie's cheeks reddened.

"We normally do not accept students in their senior year." She smiled with such haughty grandeur that Erin had to fight the temptation to curtsy. "Of course," Mrs. Keating added, "whether or not you'll be placed in the senior class will be determined by your test scores."

Erin bristled, but Cassie put an arm around her shoulders, and the pressure of her mother's fingers signaled a warning to keep quiet.

*It doesn't matter what this woman says,* Erin told herself. *I won't be coming to Windsor. I'll be making* The Dorchesters *with Abby.*

As they drove toward home, Cassie praised the school. But Erin remained silent. Finally, her mother said, "You are going to like the experience, Erin. I can promise you that. You've never known what it's like to be a normal girl attending a normal school."

"That's a normal school?"

"All right, it's not normal, and neither is your life, but you know what I mean." Cassie was flustered. "Windsor's an expensive private school, but it's an excellent one, and you'll find the girls are very friendly."

"Did you see one person smile at us? One friendly face?" Erin challenged.

"Erin, don't start an argument." Cassie struggled to control her irritation and said calmly, "The girls didn't know you, but they recognized you from television. They were cautious, that's all. You'll make many new friends when you start school in September."

As they turned into the drive to their house, Erin saw Abby's car parked at the side, and her heart began beating so loudly that she could hear it in her ears. Erin could hardly wait until her mother had stopped the car before she threw open the door on the passenger side and dashed toward the house.

As she entered the den, Abby flung her arms wide. "I got it!" she said. "It's optioned, and for six months, at least, it's ours!"

Erin shouted and hugged Abby so hard that they lost their balance and flopped onto the sofa. It was then that Erin saw Eddie standing at one side of the room.

"Hi," he said.

Erin helped Abby sit up and struggled to jump to her feet. "Hi," she said to Eddie. "I'm glad you're here."

He smiled. "I wasn't sure you would be."

"I missed you."

"I missed you, too."

"I didn't see your car outside."

"It's a dark-blue Bronco. It's parked out on the street."

"You bought the Bronco!"

"I didn't have a choice. It was going to cost too much to fix my old car."

"Excuse me," Abby said as she squirmed off the sofa and stood, straightening her skirt. "I feel as though I'm in the middle of your conversation."

Erin put a hand on Abby's arm to detain her as she began to move away. "Abby, Eddie doesn't know what we're celebrating. Do you want to tell him?"

Cassie came into the room. "Hi, Abby," she said, giving her mother a kiss. "Hi, Eddie. It's nice to see you."

"Tell Mom! Tell Eddie! Tell the whole world the great, fabulous, wonderful news!" Erin cried. She spun in a circle and wrapped her arms around herself in a hug, so excited she couldn't help laughing.

"What good news?" Cassie asked. "Mom? Have you got another TV show in the works?"

"Better than that," Erin cried. "Tell her, Abby!"

"Just give me a chance," Abby said. She beamed at Cassie. "I optioned a novel—*The Dorchesters*. I'm going to make the film."

Cassie gasped. Then she said, "Oh, Abby, that's wonderful! I read the book, and it will make a terrific film!" She stopped, looking puzzled, and added, "You've never produced a film before."

"I won't exactly produce it myself," Abby said, "unless I can't get anyone else to do it."

Cassie looked bewildered. "But you optioned it," she asked. "Who do you have in mind to star in it?"

Erin wasn't sure how much of her grandmother's indignation was real and how much was exaggerated as Abby raised her chin, stared down her nose, and answered, "*I* will star in it, Cassie, my love."

"You? As the dowager? But it's a serious drama."

"Comedy and tragedy are very closely linked," Abby said. "Believe me, I know how to make people cry as well as laugh, and not just from bad jokes."

Cassie sat down on the nearest chair. "Well, yes, but—"

"I'm not just a comic, Cassie. I'm an actress."

Erin was delighted to hear her grandmother repeating Erin's own words.

"Of course you are," Cassie answered quickly. "It's just that making and starring in a film is such a gamble." Her forehead wrinkled as she tried to remember. "What was it you said a few minutes ago about producing it if no one else would?"

"That's the next step," Abby said. "We'll have to try to get the financing we'll need."

Cassie looked shocked. "You mean you optioned the book without knowing how you'll get the film made?"

"It's done all the time. You know that."

"Yes, but by people like Robert Redford or Barbra Streisand—people who have a lot of box-office potential."

"And you think I haven't?" Abby asked with the haughty demeanor of a true dowager.

"Oh, Mom, I didn't mean it that way." Cassie stood and took her mother's hands. "You're wonderful and talented, but I was just being practical."

"There's only one way to really prove ourselves," Abby said, "and that's when the film is made and we're box-office successes."

"I believe you," Cassie began, but she suddenly stopped

and her eyes narrowed as she searched her mother's face. "You're not saying 'I.' You're saying 'we.' Who is this 'we'?"

"Erin and I," Abby said. "There's no one else who could be better cast as my granddaughter."

Cassie stepped back, her fingertips pressed against her cheeks. "Erin," she whispered, "you didn't tell me what you and Abby had plotted."

"Plotted? You make it sound so awful," Erin complained.

"You went with me to Windsor Academy, and you didn't say a word. You lied to me."

"I didn't lie!" Erin shouted.

"If you'll excuse me, I think I'd better go now," Eddie said.

"No!" Erin cried as she clutched his arm. "Don't go!" She turned to face her mother. "I did *not* lie to you! I couldn't tell you what Abby and I wanted to do until I knew if she could option the book!"

Eddie looked uncomfortable. "I mean, I shouldn't be here. This is family stuff."

Erin ignored him. "Mom, I'm an actress, too, and I don't belong in some dumb girls' school." She winced, wishing she hadn't put it like that.

"You were plotting behind my back," Cassie said, and her eyes filled with tears.

"You said it again! We weren't *plotting*! We were looking for a way in which we could advance our careers."

"The two of you deliberately kept your plan secret from me!"

Abby pressed the back of one hand against her forehead and closed her eyes. "This may be why," she said.

"Mother! Don't be so dramatic!" Cassie complained.

"Being dramatic is my job!" Abby answered.

"Do you people watch the soaps?" Eddie murmured. He succeeded in pulling his arm from Erin's grip. "I'll wait outside for you, Erin," he said, edging out of the room. "I'll be there when you cool down. I promise."

Erin burst into tears as she shouted at her mother, "You're trying to ruin my whole life!"

"By attempting to give you a normal childhood?"

"I'm not a child!"

"That's right! You've never wanted to be anything but another Abby Grant!"

"Is that so bad?" Abby asked.

"Yes!" Cassie cried. "It is for a little girl! Because of your influence, I never had a chance to show her *my* way of life."

"Your way of life?" Erin broke in before Abby could answer Cassie. "There's never been any room for me in your way. Your life consists of only two people—you and Dad. Wherever he goes, you go, and I stay home."

Cassie gasped. "But some of his locations have been in difficult places or countries where there were risks and poor medical care."

"Then you should have stayed home, too! You should have stayed with me!"

"I—I always thought it was important to be with my husband, for us not to be away from each other for long periods of time. For you, too. I've seen too many Hollywood families break up." Cassie's eyes dropped, and she looked away from her mother.

Erin rubbed away her tears with her fingertips. She took a deep breath and spoke calmly. "Why did you even have a child?"

"Oh, Erin! How can you ask that? Don't you know how much I love you?"

"No," Erin said. "If you loved me, you'd want to be with me."

Cassie held out her arms helplessly. "I couldn't be with both you and Marc." She shook her head. "But I wasn't away from you that much. Why are you dwelling on that? Can't you think about all the happy times we've had together?"

Erin nodded. "I do remember. I think about them when I try to help myself forget the other memories, the ones of my nanny holding my hand while you waved good-bye, the ones of the times when I cried myself to sleep because I missed my mother."

Cassie dropped into the nearest chair and buried her head in her arms. "I tried so hard not to make mistakes," she said.

Abby crossed the room and put a hand on her daughter's shoulder. "All mothers make mistakes," she said, "no matter how hard they try not to."

Cassie reached for her mother's hand and held it tightly without raising her head. "I wanted Erin to have a happy life," she said.

"Haven't you noticed? She *is* happy," Abby said.

"Not with her mother."

"With her *life*, and that's what counts, isn't it? She's happy being an actress."

Cassie sat up and looked at Abby. "But I've seen what being an actress has done to *you*. You've had successes, but you've had so many terrible disappointments, too—like with your variety show. I want Erin to have a more stable life, not one that's a series of ups and downs."

Erin dropped to her knees next to her mother's chair. "Mom, everybody has ups and downs. It hurt me a lot when *The Family Next Door* was ended, and it hurt when Gene and Lydia didn't call me. They were like my parents, too, and they didn't even call me to say good-bye."

Cassie flinched, but she said, "Erin, that's part of what I mean."

"But it isn't," Erin said. "I shouldn't have brought up Lydia and Gene. I was just trying to show you that I can take the downs when they come. And in the long run, it's not the hurting times that matter. It's the successes that count. Look at Abby. Her whole life has been a success."

"Don't talk about my life in the past tense," Abby said. "I'm looking forward to the future. I'm going to make a film."

"You're taking a big risk," Cassie warned.

"But that's the point! It's the risk-taking that makes life so exciting."

"For me, too, Mom," Erin said.

"And what if the film is . . . what if it isn't well-received?"

"Go ahead and say it. What if it's a bomb? Well, if it is, so be it," Abby said. "But we have to be positive from the start that it won't be."

"That's right," Erin said. "We have to believe in ourselves. I know that no one else could play that part as well as Abby."

"And no one else would be as perfect for the grand-daughter as Erin," Abby added. "You've got to admit it will have commercial appeal."

Cassie fumbled in her skirt pocket and found a tissue. She mopped at her eyes and took a long, deep breath. "All right," she said. "Let's talk. You've optioned the book. What comes next?"

"Going the route I mentioned, with studios first," Abby said. "If the studios won't come through, we'll try to get a package together—script, director, and so forth—and try to find investors."

"It's going to be hard," Cassie said. "They'll all see you as a comic, Mom, not as a serious actress. You have to face facts. They'll remember what you did last—the variety show that failed."

"That's their problem," Abby said.

Cassie was silent for a moment, and Erin began to fidget.

"You haven't told me yet," she said to Cassie. "Will you let me be in the film?"

"I'll make a deal with you," Cassie said. "You'll take the placement tests next week for Windsor Academy, just as Mrs. Keating arranged. If Abby finds someone to come up with the funds for the film before September, you can take the role and work with a studio teacher. If Abby doesn't get the funding by then, you'll start Windsor Academy in the fall semester."

"But Abby has a six-month option! It's less than five months until September."

"One month won't make that much difference."

"You said yourself, it might be hard to convince investors that Abby could play that part."

"Take the offer," Abby advised. "Remember, we have to keep believing in ourselves."

"Okay," Erin muttered. "I'll take it." A chill gripped her backbone, and she couldn't help shivering. It wasn't just a matter of Abby and Erin believing in themselves. It was other people—people with investment money—who had to believe in them, too.

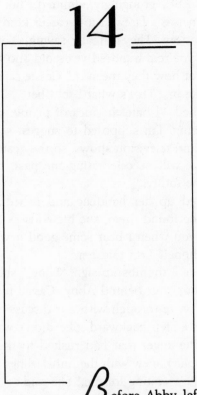

# 14

*B*efore Abby left, she said to Cassie, "This is probably a rotten time to bring it up, but how'd you like to give a little speech and say something nice about me?" She told Cassie about the dinner in May at which she'd be honored.

"Oh, Mom, I'm honored that you'd ask me," Cassie said, and her eyes shone. "What a wonderful tribute they're giving you!"

"Maybe," Abby grudgingly admitted, "but I keep think-ing of the dinner as a farewell-to-a-career kind of affair. You know what I mean. They're really saying, 'You did a good job, and now you're a hundred years old and it's over.' "

"That's not how they mean it," Cassie said.

Erin broke in. "That's what I told her."

Abby sighed. "I hate the idea of people sitting around and remembering. I'm supposed to suggest selections from favorite films and television shows, so they can put together a program that will be celebrating the past, but I'd rather think about the future."

She picked up her handbag and fished in it for her keys. When she found them, she blew kisses to Cassie and Erin. "I'll call you when I hear some good news," she said.

"Soon, I hope!" Erin told her.

Abby made a thumbs-up sign. "Soon," she said.

As the door shut behind Abby, Cassie turned to Erin. "I don't think we're through with our discussion," she said.

Erin took a step backward. She didn't want to talk to her mother. The anger that had rushed to the surface was still there, bubbling anew with the hurt feelings that wouldn't go away. "Eddie's waiting for me," she said.

Cassie slumped against the door. "I thought it would be easier now."

"It's never going to be easy."

Erin fidgeted uncomfortably until her mother said, "Go ahead, then. I suppose Eddie's been waiting for you long enough."

Eddie was sitting in the shade near the swimming pool. He jumped to his feet when he heard Erin's footsteps and wrapped his arms around her. "I thought you'd forgotten me," he said.

"Never," Erin answered, and kissed him with all the hunger and loneliness and regret she'd suffered since their last parting.

Eddie came up for air long enough to say, "That answers the question."

"I'm sorry," Erin murmured, "for not saying 'thank you' at the zoo. I didn't mean to act like a spoiled brat."

"Typecasting," Eddie mumbled against her lips, and kissed her again.

Less than five minutes later, Eddie said, "I can't stay any longer, Erin."

Erin, submerged in emotions she had never experienced before, was reluctant to let him go. "No. Stay with me. I don't want you to leave," she insisted.

Eddie stepped back and tried to read his watch by the lights around the pool. "I haven't got a choice," he said. "I've got a job to get to."

It was hard for Erin to come back to reality. "A—A job?" she stammered. "That's great! What is it? TV? A movie? A commercial?"

Eddie laughed and put an arm around her shoulders, hugging her to his side. "It's not what you think, Erin. There's another world out there. Not everyone is in front of a camera."

"I just thought—"

"I'm doing some promotion work, as Clarence Nutweilder, for a gift store in the mall down on Santa Monica. It's only for this week, but it helps pay the bills."

He held out a hand. "Come with me to see my new car. I parked it out on the street."

She slipped her hand into his and followed him out of the patio and down the drive.

Erin inspected the car closely, admiring it while Eddie beamed. However, her mind was not on the highly polished Bronco, but on Eddie. She couldn't understand her emotions. She had never felt like this about any boy—this wild hunger to cling to him, to press her mouth against his, to never let him go.

She suddenly took a step toward him. "When will I see you again?" she murmured.

He came close, looking down into her eyes. "I'll be back," he said, and kissed her lightly, his lips scarcely brushing her own.

*Eddie's my friend. My good friend, my best friend, my only real friend. What is going to happen to our friendship?* There were too many reasons why a serious love would be wrong for now. She was too young for a commitment, and she knew that no matter how she felt about Eddie, or anyone, her career would have to come first. Wishing life didn't have to be so complicated, Erin watched Eddie drive away.

Abby had said she'd be in touch with good news soon, but it wasn't soon. As the days went by, Abby had nothing positive to report. "The studios just can't see me as Judith Dorchester," Abby told Erin over the phone. "I've also talked to a couple of the independent production companies, and they aren't the least bit encouraging. In fact, I'm pretty sure that one of them is just waiting for my option to run out so they can pick up the book. I suspect they have a big-name star all lined up."

"Who?"

"I couldn't find out. They're pretty tight-lipped about her."

A sudden lump of fear tightened Erin's stomach. "Nobody else can make that film!" she cried.

"I agree with you," Abby said, "so I'll keep trying. We may have to put together a package. I have a writer in mind, and I'll see what it will cost to have a script written. I'm guessing at least a hundred thousand. And, of course, we'll have to get a definite commitment from a well-known director."

"Abby!" Erin cried. "We've got a director! Dad could do it!"

"Calm down," Abby said. "I've already thought of your father, even though he directs *films* instead of movies." She dropped the sarcasm and added, "Marc is a very popular director, Erin. We're not going to ask him to turn down something lucrative from a major studio to gamble on our wild shot. Understand?"

"Yes," Erin said, and she frantically began grasping for other ideas. "Mom and Dad have put most of my salary aside. Let me see if they'll allow me to borrow against it."

"Uh-uh. That won't work. The state of California has laws to protect your income. Don't worry. I can always call on my friendly neighborhood banker." Abby paused, then added, "Yesterday, Mary Lou mailed me a check. It won't cover the cost of the script, but it's a big help."

Erin's worry left with a rush. That check was of more help than Mary Lou had known. "Abby, there are lots of people who love you and believe in you," Erin said. "I'm more positive than ever now. It's all going to work out."

As she hung up the receiver, she heard Cassie calling her to dinner, so Erin sprinted to the dining room, seated herself in her usual place between her parents, and flicked her napkin onto her lap.

She still felt uncomfortable when she was with her mother. Their argument hadn't cleared the air or settled the problem between them. If anything, it had made things worse. And Erin had made excuses every time her mother had suggested they continue the talk and try to work things out.

Erin didn't want to. Cassie had proved that she hadn't really understood how much Erin's career meant to her—not when she had hung that threat of Windsor Academy over Erin's head. Erin's hurt feelings were like a shriveled, drying scab that she couldn't leave alone.

"Erin? I asked you a question."

It dawned on Erin that her father was speaking to her. "I'm sorry," she said. "I was thinking about something."

"Remember, I'd said I might have a surprise for you and your mother? Well, I do. I've got an unexpected break, and I thought we all might want to take a long vacation somewhere. Hawaii? Paris? The Greek Isles? You name it."

"Why do you have an unexpected break?" Erin asked slowly.

"Why?" Her father looked puzzled. "Well, it happens that I'd agreed to direct a film for Martin James, but there were some legal problems and it's been delayed indefinitely."

Erin dropped her fork and stared at her father. "Dad!" she said. "That's fantastic! You could direct *The Dorchesters!*"

For an instant, Marc's jaw dropped in surprise. He sat up a little taller in his chair, shook his head firmly, and said, "Erin, that's impossible."

"Why is it impossible? You're a great director, Dad, and you could do a terrific job."

"Abby hasn't got a producer. She hasn't got the backing."

"But she *will* have! She's putting together a package to take to the investment groups. If they knew you were going to be the director, it would make a big difference."

Marc sighed and closed his eyes for a moment. When he opened them, he said, "Abby built a fantastic reputation as a comedienne. She's typecast in the public's mind. It's going to be hard for people to accept her in a serious role."

"Are you saying you won't do it because you think our movie is going to be a bomb?"

"That's a little harsh. . . . Okay, yes, that's one reason, but there are others. Have you given any consideration to the tremendous cost of making the film and the financial risks involved?"

Erin slumped in her chair. "Abby's not afraid to try something new, because she knows she can do a good job. And with a great director, it could be an outstanding job." She looked up at her father. "Didn't you ever take a risk? Didn't you ever go for something you wanted to do even though people said they didn't think you could do it?"

"Yes, he has," Cassie said.

Marc looked at Cassie, and a strange expression came

over his face. "That's right. I did take a very big risk once," he said. "It was my first film, and your mother starred in it, even though Abby was very much against it."

Erin was startled. "Mom was an *actress*?"

"Once. Just once," Cassie told her. "That was enough for me."

"You never told me. What film was it? Why haven't I seen it?"

Cassie laughed. "You can see it. We'll run it for you some time. It wasn't a full-length feature, only a short, and your father made it while he was a student at USC in an attempt to win an apprenticeship with a famous director."

"Did he?"

"No, but the film attracted the attention of other directors, who became interested in his work."

While Erin tried with difficulty to picture her mother as an actress, she suddenly remembered the rest of what her father had told her. "Wait a minute," she said to Marc. "You said that Abby was against it."

"That's right."

"Mom acted in it anyway?"

Erin turned her gaze on her mother, who blushed as she nodded.

"Very interesting," Erin said, enjoying Cassie's discomfort. She looked back at Marc. "Did you produce the film all by yourself?"

"Essentially."

"How did you do it? Didn't anyone help you make it, or publicize it, or distribute it?"

One corner of Marc's mouth turned up in a twisted smile. "As a matter of fact, someone did step in. . . . Abby."

Erin was even more intrigued. She wanted to hear the rest of the story, but this wasn't the time. "Then why don't you help Abby now?" she said.

"There are other factors to consider," Marc told Erin. "Whether or not Abby can carry it off is almost beside the point. Your mother wants you to experience a life outside the field of acting. If I told you I'd direct this film, if I helped it to be made, I'd be working against her wishes."

Erin had opened her mouth to protest when she heard her mother say, "Marc, I was close to Erin's age when I knew what I wanted out of life. It was so simple, so black and white. I wanted to be a photographer, and I wanted you. And I would have defied everyone in heaven and earth, including my mother, to get what I wanted."

As Erin stared at her mother in amazement, Cassie said, "I'd forgotten what it was like to be so young, to be so sure of my goals." She reached out a hand and placed it over Erin's, but her eyes were on her husband. "Marc," she said, "as a favor to me, will you please direct Abby's and Erin's film?"

Marc gave Cassie the special look that had always made Erin feel like an intruder. Then he said, "If you want me to, Cass, I will."

Erin looked at her mother as though she were seeing a stranger, someone she hadn't known before, a beautiful, pale-haired woman with such open yearning in her eyes that Erin's throat tightened.

Her mother's hand turned, grasping Erin's, as she told her, "Maybe I can help make things up to you, Erin. I've always worked at having the perfect marriage. I thought that was the best gift I could give you. I never in the world would have believed that I'd made you feel left out."

"Oh, Mom!" Erin cried, and with a rush of love she jumped from her chair and wrapped her arms around her mother. "I'm sorry for all the things I said to you. I didn't understand either. I didn't even try."

It was Marc who interrupted as their tears began to subside. "What do you say we call Abby?" he asked. "I'll offer to direct *The Dorchesters*. We'll see what she has to say."

Marc relayed his offer, then held the phone away from his ear. Erin could hear Abby's loud whoop of laughter.

"That makes it perfect!" Abby shouted. "Come over, all of you! Come right now!"

"What is it?" Erin asked her father.

"I guess we'll have to wait to find out when we get there," he said.

As Mrs. Jefferson ushered them into Abby's sun room, Erin was surprised to see that Abby was not alone. Uncle Bobby and an elderly man in a European-styled, pale wool suit turned to greet them. Bobby's face was alight with the same anticipatory smile Erin saw on his face each Christmas Eve before she'd opened the beautifully wrapped packages he'd brought for her.

Abby, the long, wide sleeves of her embroidered Mexican dress swooping like sails as she gestured, chortled with delight as she completed the introductions. "Our director,

Marc Jenkins," she said, flinging an arm around Marc's shoulders. With her other hand, she gestured toward the man in the expensive suit. "And our backer, Carlo Valenta."

Erin jumped and let out a squeal. "We can go ahead? We can make the film?"

With an airy wave, as though she were dismissing trivialities, Abby said, "Oh, we'll have to go through attorneys and tax specialists and work out an arrangement with a production company and all of that, but the answer is yes. Thanks to Mr. Valenta and Bobby, we can make *The Dorchesters.*"

Mr. Valenta clapped a hand on Bobby's shoulder. "When I discovered that my friend Bobby Baynes was related to Abby Grant, and Abby Grant needed money to make a picture, I considered it my lucky day. I'm bored with my restaurant chain. I'm bored with my sons who have taken it over. 'Retire, Papa,' they told me. 'Enjoy some of those millions you've made.' So I tried, but everything I did was boring. Even the racetrack got to be boring."

*So that's where Uncle Bobby met him,* Erin thought.

Mr. Valenta's eyes brightened. "But making a movie is not boring. It's exciting, and I have always been in love with Abby Grant."

Bobby tried to look modest. "Whenever Abby needs me, I come through," he said. He looked to his sister for confirmation. "Isn't that right, Abby?"

"That's right, Bobby," she said, "and you really outdid yourself this time."

The conversation swelled around Erin like bright balloons, but her mind wasn't on it. All she could think, over and over, was, *We're going to film* The Dorchesters!

Eventually, Abby, Bobby, and Mr. Valenta left to have dinner at the Bel Age, and Erin and her parents drove home.

In the car, Erin wondered how it was possible to be so happy. "Isn't it wonderful!" she cried.

Her father chuckled. "Imagine Bobby as the one who came up with investment funds. It's certainly fitting after all these years in which Abby's had to take care of him."

"Hush," Cassie said, and threw a quick glance at Erin in the backseat.

Erin just grinned. She was delighted that Bobby finally had done something to be proud of. He'd tell the story over and over, adding details, for years to come, but she didn't mind. It was worth it. "No problem," she said.

"There is a problem," her father said. "And it's not a small one."

"But we've got the backing—"

"We're going to need something else just as much, and that's box-office receipts. It's not just the money that will be invested in this film. Our reputations will be on the line. If people won't accept Abby in a serious role, they won't buy tickets to see the film."

"They *will* accept her. There'll be the previews of coming attractions in the movie theaters."

Cassie shook her head. "I don't think the previews would be enough. They'd not only show too little, but they'd appear too close to the release of the film. The film critics have preconceived ideas about Abby, and even Marc's strong reputation may not be enough. We'll need them on our side long before that, so they can tout the film and prepare the public. And we'll need distributors on our side, too."

"*We'll* need." "*Our* side." Erin was warmed by her mother's words. It was no longer Abby and Erin against Cassie. It was the three of them together, all with the same goal. She smiled as she imagined herself and her mother at Abby's testimonial dinner, praising Abby not only for what she'd accomplished, but for what lay ahead.

"Dad!" she shouted so loudly that her father jumped and the car swerved. "I've got the answer!"

# 15

$\mathcal{A}$t Marc's insistence, Erin
waited until they arrived home before she laid out her plan.

"Abby isn't completely happy with the testimonial banquet, because it celebrates her past. She said she'd rather look toward the future."

Cassie nodded agreement, and Erin continued. "There'll be over a thousand people connected with film and television at the banquet, and some of them will be with the press. So, Dad, why couldn't we film one of the most dramatic scenes from the film—enough so people could get caught up in the emotions—and show it to them instead of those film clips from her past? We could give them a taste of *The Dorchesters* and of Abby's future."

Marc stood up and began to walk, as he often did when he wanted to think through an idea. "We can't just take a scene from the film," he said. "We won't be into production by the time the banquet takes place. How much time have we got—three, four weeks?"

"Four," Cassie said.

"It doesn't have to be a scene from the film," Erin insisted. "We could choose one scene from the story and hire someone to write just that part of the script. We could put together a set, and it wouldn't have to be the one we'd use in the film. We could even use our den, or Abby's sun room."

"One scene," Marc repeated, and rubbed his chin.

"Maybe the scene in which Judith's secret comes out," Erin suggested. "That's really dramatic."

"No." Cassie stood and looked down at Erin. "That scene would give too much away. We want to show the audience an intriguing teaser that will have them wanting to see more. There's a much better scene in that book."

"What's that?" Erin asked.

"The scene in which the conflict between Judith Dorchester and her granddaughter reaches a peak and explodes and Judith strikes Kim. It was written so vividly, I could see it—the instant loss of control, the shock, the remorse that Judith refuses to speak, and Kim's cold anger as she defies her grandmother. I got chills as I read it."

Marc let out a low whistle. "Where's the book?" he asked. "I'm ready to read it."

Erin ran up the stairs to get the novel. Just as she was entering her bedroom, the phone rang, and she hurried to answer it.

"Hi," Eddie said.

At the sound of his voice, Erin's heart began pounding. "I'm glad it's you," she said.

"Are you?" He sounded pleased. "I called because I've got two questions for you. One, when can I see you? Tonight? Tomorrow? And two, will you and your family be under control?"

Erin laughed. "The problem's been worked out, and things couldn't be better."

He hesitated. "I hope that comes with a guarantee."

"I was going to call you," Erin said, "because I've got some good news to tell you. And you're not the only one with questions. I've got one to ask you."

"What is it?"

"Come over now," she said. "Can you? I'll ask you when I see you."

"Okay," he said. "I'll be there in fifteen minutes."

Erin watched for Eddie's car, and when she saw headlights swing into their driveway, she ran outside to meet him.

As Eddie climbed down from his Bronco, Erin paused, gulped, and blurted out, "Eddie, you're my good friend, so you know what I'm like, and what I want, and it's okay with you. Right?"

Erin could hear the smile in Eddie's voice. "Erin, we don't have to look at life the same way. You're interesting, you're funny, maybe a little off the wall sometimes, but that's the way you are, and that's the way I want you to be."

Erin gave a long, happy sigh. "I'm glad that was your answer, because I've found the answer to another question . . . one I asked myself a while ago."

"What was that?"

"I wondered," Erin said, "if it was okay to fall in love with a good friend." She stepped close to Eddie and wrapped her arms around his neck. "And it is. . . . It definitely—" Whatever else Erin had planned to say was lost in the eagerness of Eddie's kiss.

Erin had never worked as hard as she had during the past few weeks. Her father demanded perfection, and she and Abby had to go through take after take after take.

"We won't finish in time!" she complained, thinking if the slate was snapped in front of her face just once more she'd scream.

"We'll finish," her father said calmly, "if you get closer inside your character. Think about it. The hate is churning within you, burning your chest, rising in your throat to choke you. You look at your grandmother, and the hate spills out of your eyes. Think, Erin. Feel it. Now we're going to do it one more time."

Marc refused to allow Abby, Cassie, and Erin to see the daily rushes. Finally, he ran the finished scene for them.

*192*

"That was really us?" Erin whispered as the lights in the screening room came up.

"Go ahead. Say it." Abby's voice was husky, almost breathless. "We were terrific. Oscar material, if I do say so myself."

Marc beamed at them. "You were fantastic—both of you." He put an arm around Erin's shoulders. "You're as talented an actress as your grandmother. I can't possibly give you a greater compliment than that."

Cassie wiped tears from her eyes. "I guess I've never really been aware of how very talented the two of you are."

"You're every bit as good, Cassie," Abby said. "I can still remember the amazement I felt—even a little awe—at your one venture as an actress."

Cassie's eyes shone. "You *were* proud of me, weren't you?"

"Of course I was. Very proud."

"That was important to me," Cassie said. "In spite of rebelling against you, I really wanted to please you."

Erin looked at her mother and quietly said, "That's the way I feel, too. These past four years, I've wanted you to see me, see how good I really am."

"Oh!" Cassie cried. "Erin! You should know how proud I am of you. I love you."

"It was the same for me," Abby said in a distant voice. "From the time I was a little girl, I wanted most to please my mother." She smiled and added, "But at the same time, we're all so darned independent, when we've got a goal in mind there's only one thing to do and that's go for it, mother or no mother."

Erin laughed. "Like *The Dorchesters.*"

"Let's not give ourselves all the credit for that scene." Abby looked up at Marc. "You brought it off, Marc."

"It's just the beginning," he said. "We've got an entire film to make. This is just the teaser, as Cassie pointed out."

"The people at the banquet, the critics—they've got to like it," Erin said.

But she couldn't help being scared.

The night of the banquet, Erin poked at the food on her plate, unable to eat a bite or chat much with Eddie, who was seated next to her. She found it hard to keep her mind on the toasts to Abby and the speeches, and her hands were trembling when she and Cassie got up to stand with Abby at the microphones.

Their short tributes to Abby went well. The applause was enthusiastic. Then Cassie held up a hand for silence.

This was it. Now Erin would find out how their film would be accepted—*if* it would be accepted.

"The original plan," Cassie said to the audience, "was to show clips from my mother's most successful films and television shows, but Abby has never been one to look back, to dwell on what has happened when it's so much more interesting to think about what's *going* to happen. So you'll be the first to see a scene from Abby's film in progress, *The Dorchesters,* and you're going to see an Abby Grant who doesn't stop to look back but who moves her career in new and exciting directions—always forward."

There was murmuring as a large screen rolled down at one end of the room, the lights were turned off, and the film began. Marc had wanted no opening title or credits, just the countdown numbers leading into the scene. As Abby's face, lined and devoid of most of the heavy makeup she was noted for, appeared on the screen, a few people in the large banquet room laughed, and Erin sucked in her breath.

But as the Abby on the screen began to speak, her words raw and brittle with fury, the audience hushed. Erin became caught up in the scene again, but she was still aware that there was absolute silence in the huge room. No coughing, no sounds of movement—it was almost as though no one dared to breathe.

In just a few minutes the scene was over, and the lights came on. Erin expected the guests to applaud, but they didn't. No one moved.

Erin wanted to cry out, "Don't do this to Abby! Couldn't you see how good she was in that role? What's the matter with all of you?"

Then the room exploded. People jumped to their feet, applauding and cheering.

"Mom! Erin!" Cassie cried over the noise as she hugged them. "You're getting a standing ovation!"

"I've had them before," Abby said, but she winked conspiratorily at Erin. Like a queen, she held out her hands to her admirers and moved into the crowd that was swarming toward her.

A group of red-jacketed waiters was herded quickly into the room to finish clearing the tables. A very young waiter, edging through the crowd, sidestepped the growing mob around Abby, but as he turned to stare, he collided with Erin. He grabbed her shoulder, helping her to regain her balance, and did a double take.

"Hey!" he said. "I know you. You're Katie Norman on *The Family Next Door.*"

Erin smiled. "Not anymore."

He looked puzzled for a moment, then glanced back at Abby. "Well, I know who *she* is," he said, frowning as he tried to recall the name. "Didn't she used to be Abby . . . uh, Abby . . . ?"

"She's Abby Grant," Erin told him, poking his shoulder at each word for emphasis, "and I'm Erin Jenkins. Remember those names. You're going to be hearing them for a long, long time!"

# About the Author

JOAN LOWERY NIXON is the acclaimed author of more than eighty books for children and young adults. She is a three-time winner of Mystery Writers of America's Edgar Award and the recipient of many Children's Choice awards. Her other popular books for young adults include *The Other Side of Dark*, *The Kidnapping of Christina Lattimore*, and *The Seance*, as well as the books in the Orphan Train Quartet: *A Family Apart*, *Caught in the Act*, *In the Face of Danger*, and *A Place to Belong*.

Mrs. Nixon and her husband live in Houston, Texas.